THE ROMA NOVA THRILLERS
The Carina Mitela adventures
INCEPTIO
CARINA (novella)
PERFIDITAS
SUCCESSIO

The Aurelia Mitela adventures
AURELIA
INSURRECTIO
RETALIO

ROMA NOVA EXTRA (Short stories)

———

ABOUT THE AUTHOR

A 'Roman nut' since age 11, Alison Morton has clambered over much of Roman Europe; she continues to be fascinated by that complex, powerful and value driven civilisation.

Armed with an MA in history, six years' military service and a love of thrillers, she explores via her Roma Nova novels the 'what if' idea of a modern Roman society run by strong women.

Alison lives in France with her husband, cultivates a Roman herb garden and drinks wine.

Find out more at alison-morton.com, follow her on Twitter @alison_morton and Facebook (AlisonMortonAuthor)

·CARINA·

ALISON MORTON

PULCHERIA
PRESS

ISBN 9791097310066

DRAMATIS PERSONAE

Family
Carina Mitela – Lieutenant, Praetorian Guard Special Forces (PGSF)
Conradus Mitelus – Major, PGSF, Carina's husband
Aurelia Mitela – Carina's grandmother, head of Mitela family
Helena Mitela – Carina's cousin
Allegra Mitela – Carina and Conrad's daughter

Military
Daniel Stern – Lieutenant, PGSF
Flavius – Optio, PGSF, part of Carina's Active Response Team
Lucius – Adjutant, PGSF
Granius – Cypher clerk, Praetorian Guard
Dubnus – Guard, PGSF
Fausta – IT specialist
Murria – Lieutenant, Interrogation Service
Vara – PGSF legate
Atria – Optio, PGSF, part of Carina's Active Response Team
Livius – Optio, PGSF, part of Carina's Active Response Team

Other
Marcia Vibiana – a renegade scientist
Hayden Black – owner, Bornes & Black Advertising Agency
Special Agent O'Keefe – FBI, New York
Inspector Cornelius Lurio – Department of Justice *custodes*
Prisca Monticola – head of the Roma Nova Silver Guild

1

'I should flay you both for this. It's a bloody good job we're not back in the Ancients' times. A good Roman punishment officer would have sorted you both out.'

I winced at the laser-like words.

'I can see no reason why I shouldn't throw you both out this instant. You've disobeyed standing orders, your reckless behaviour has set an extremely poor example to all ranks and it would be a complete waste of your expensive training if you'd broken your stupid necks.'

It was Daniel's fault we were standing here getting the biggest bollocking ever. He'd dared me to a bare-hand climbing race up the inner courtyard wall of the old fortress building. Strictly forbidden because the stonework was loose and flaking after eight hundred years, but I couldn't resist the challenging sparkle in his eye. And being November, ice had formed overnight in the old limestone mortar cracks adding to the danger.

Of course, we got an audience; of course, they made book on us, but the shouts of encouragement and even the catcalls spurred us both on.

Halfway up, one piece of stone came away in my half-frozen hand. I let it fall to the ground which caused more shouting, a few laughs and some cursing. That bastard Dubnus shook his fist at me, egging on his group of buddies with filthy comments.

We'd reached the top, neck and neck, muscles trembling and breath heaving. I had the tiniest margin on Daniel. One last effort and I pulled myself up, my stomach on the edge of the crumbling parapet and swung myself over. I'd hardly flung my arms up in victory when the shouting died at a stroke.

A voice like a shotgun had rung out, ordering us down that instant. Major Mitelus, our commander, was incandescent. Even from five storeys up I could see his hazel eyes were blazing.

'Oh, shit,' Daniel said softly, then coughed. His lungs grasped air from the cool November morning.

'Squared,' I said. 'What the hell is he doing here anyway? He wasn't due in until the afternoon.'

'Well, you'd know.'

Major Mitelus was also my husband, Conrad. Something which made my life more than difficult.

His eyes were still blazing now thirty minutes later as Daniel and I stood rigid as funeral *imagines* in front of his desk. As well as my hands burning from the warmth inside the building, my heart was hammering harder than when I'd been at the top of our climb.

'I will not tolerate such behaviour from my junior officers. It reflects poorly on the unit and the senior staff. Mars knows we don't need any more more problems at the moment.' He shot an incinerating look at me. He'd mentioned at home only the night before that he was fending off subtle attempts to stop his pending promotion, move him out of his post and put one of the legate's cronies in his place. The warmth crept up my neck but I couldn't think of anything to say.

'Badges on my desk, and empty your pockets.'

Car keys, pen, notepad, phone, locker key and a few *solidi* from me; pretty near the same from Daniel.

'Earpiece, too.' Hades. Without that part the tooth mic would be useless.

He nodded at the security detail who grasped our arms.

'Seven days in the cells.'

I pulled against the hand gripping my arm and took half a step forward.

'You can't—'

'Take them down,' he said and looked away.

The bastard. Not for the punishment. I guess that was due. No, now I would miss our daughter's fourth birthday.

'Books,' the guard grumped and thrust them at me. I caught them in my arms before they fell on the cell floor. 'She'll bring more in a couple of days,' he said over his shoulder as he went out before I could ask who had brought them. The heavy metal door clanged shut.

I stared at the smooth grey surface only broken by the observation panel, handle and lock. It was the barrier to seeing Allegra, my daughter, walk towards the family altar, be guided up the step by my cousin Helena instead of me.

Allegra's little fingers would drop the incense on the altar as a sacrifice to her *genius*, the tutelary spirit that would guide and protect her for the next year. She'd flinch as the flames flared and then probably wipe her fingers on her white dress. Helena would give her a quick hug, help her down, take her hand and find her a drink. My grandmother, Aurelia, would kiss her great-grandchild and they'd all devour cake. Perhaps Allegra would ask where Mama was. I kicked the door in frustration, cursing the plastic sandals I now wore that gave my toes no protection.

I looked at the books. A mix of light adventure and historical romances. A slight bulge in the pages of one revealed a note. *Shit luck you caught this for Allegra's birthday. Hope these help pass the time. H.* Helena, my cousin and friend. Thank you, I breathed.

The very worst was the boredom. Then the lack of exercise. I stomped up and down my cell every day for an hour morning and evening, inventing new curses for Conrad. He was my commanding officer. I knew he was correct, but I still thought it was unfair. My fists balled during my pacing for the first two days. I merely strode the next two. By day six, I had relaxed my shoulders and when, thank Juno, the door opened on the morning of the eighth day, I had accepted it. I wasn't happy, but I'd accepted it.

Daniel grinned at me as he stood in the corridor waiting for me after he'd been let out of his cell.

'Are you okay?' he asked.

'Fabulous,' I replied.

'That bad?'

'Huh.'

'Drink later?'

'Yes. And let's get smashed.'

After being released from the custody suite at 7 a.m., where the duty sergeant gave me a smirk along with a sealed plastic bag containing my uniform, crowned eagle badge and other stuff, I checked my duty note, relieved to find I wasn't rostered until the afternoon. Ignoring the sly grins from some in the unit, I smiled back at those who smiled at me or gave me a comradely pat on the back or arm.

At home, I tried to sneak in through the service entrance, but had the humiliation of waiting like a peddler until one of the house security team let me in. After seven days out, my password sync with the house system was completely invalid. I crept up the backstairs and after a shower and change of clothes, I headed for the nursery and folded Allegra into my arms.

'Lo, Mama.' She gave me a wet kiss and pushed herself against my body. Tears welled in my eyes. I sat down, still clutching her to me.

'Mama is very sorry she wasn't here for your birthday.'

'Allegra loves Mama,' she said, copper-brown lights overcoming the green in her hazel eyes, the twins of her father's. I gripped her, her face warm against the skin of my neck. Even if I had another ten children – the gods forbid – she would always be the child of my heart.

'Well, we toasted absent friends,' came a clipped voice. I stood, still holding Allegra, and saw Helena. Perfect as always, even in a sweater and jeans. Her smooth skin, immaculately made up, and hair caught up in elaborate braids at the back of her head and not one hair out of place made her look like a model. She had the same Mitela blue eyes as many women in my family did, and I could see her resemblance, but softer, to my grandmother. But she had poise, that indefinable body confidence I'd never achieve.

'Thank you for looking after Allegra on her birthday,' I said.

'Yes, that was crap timing.'

'Well, it wasn't intentional,' I fired back. Allegra gripped my neck harder.

'That wasn't what Conrad said. He was as cross as Jupiter on a bad

4

day. He kept it in for Allegra's sake, but afterwards, he threw almost a full tumbler of whisky down his throat and told us exactly what had happened.' She frowned at me. 'How could you do something so stupid?'

I didn't answer. I stared at her. Helena would never understand that spark that pushed us on in the military, why we felt the challenge and the need to answer it. And being in the Praetorian Guard Special Forces doubled, even trebled it. She'd never been in uniform; they'd abolished national service back in the nineties. Allegra squirmed in my arms, so I set her down among the cushions.

'Aurelia said she wanted to see you as soon as you'd finished here.' Helena looked at me with a steady gaze. 'You'd better put a fireproof suit on first.'

2

My grandmother was sitting at her desk in the *tablinum*, her formal office just off the atrium. Her head bowed over a file and pen hovered a centimetre or two above it. I shut the door behind me and went to speak.

'One moment,' she said without looking up.

I stood there, somehow feeling I shouldn't sit down before I was invited. That was ridiculous. This was my beloved Nonna who had welcomed me when I'd fled to Roma Nova, who had given me a home and supported me from average girl to the Praetorian officer I was now. But in her formal work suit, her gold-rimmed spectacles perched on her nose, her attention one hundred per cent on her file – one of a pile on her desk – she looked every bit the formidable senator and imperial councillor she was.

She looked up at last and leant back in her carved chair.

'I expect Conrad has barked at you and Helena will no doubt have made you feel guilty.' Her voice was flat. 'I'm not going to add to that, but I would like you to consider what impact you may have had on the reputation of the family.' She pushed a newspaper across the desk. My face and large headlines.

Stupid or brave?

Young Mitela heir nearly kills herself for a bet.

Is this what we expect from the senior of the Twelve Families?

'How did they find out?' I said, appalled at the tabloid.

'Don't be naive, Carina,' she snapped. 'The journalists are always sniffing around. Some loose tongue mentioned it in a bar and it flared round at the speed of light.' She sighed. 'None of us has a perfect record. When I was framed for murder in Prussia forty years ago, the news got out, but the foreign ministry managed to damp it down. These days, if you sneeze, digital cameras and the Internet will have you dying of flu within minutes.'

I swallowed hard.

'This piece is five days old now. Luckily, your time in the cells will have let the whole thing quieten down. I suggest you don't go to any events in the city for a few days. Do your duty shifts, then come straight home. You need to get back into your routine.' She looked at her watch. 'Now I must get on.' She bent her head back to her work.

I was dismissed, but so flooded with embarrassment I couldn't move. Underneath I resented being treated like a rebellious teenager. I was a grown woman of twenty-nine, for the gods' sake. She was the head of the family, but how could she close me out like this? She had to listen to my side of it.

'I'm sorry, Nonna, if my conduct has reflected badly on you, but—'

'Apology accepted,' she interrupted and looked up. 'But it's not on me. A few snide remarks before the Senate session are nothing.' She fixed me with her eyes. 'It's the family. I try to keep them in line, stop them doing stupid things, rescuing them when they do. I can't keep my eye on several hundred cousins all the time, though. However, I do expect the closest members of my household to behave and especially my heir.'

'I—'

'No, not another word, Carina. Just go and get on and try to live this down.'

She went back to her work and, still smarting, I made for the door.

There was no way I was going to the canteen at the barracks for lunch, so I grabbed a sandwich from the machine and made myself a cup of coffee in the tiny kitchen off our corridor. Ignoring the twenty or so other juniors in the open general office, I negotiated my way to my shabby desk. After fielding the mountain of messages on my screen and the sticky notes curling at the edge on my desk, most irrelevant now, I sighed at my in tray. I'd missed giving a weapons training exercise, but I saw a pinned note on the file that a colleague had covered it for me.

'Mitela!'

Crap, Lucius, the adjutant. His hand rested on the door and he was frowning at me. He jerked his head at me then turned and left. I hurried across the general office to the door, weaving in between the desks. Out in the corridor, I saw him disappear into his room, but leaving the door open.

'Well, you covered yourself in glory this time, didn't you?'

I said nothing as I stood in front of his desk.

'Oh, sit down and stop looking like an offended pigeon.'

I perched on the edge of the plastic padded chair and waited for more scathing words.

'I expect you've had enough bollocking, so I won't add to it.' He grinned. 'I'll have your hide if you tell Conradus, but I made fifty *solidi* on the book.'

I gave him a weak smile.

'I suggested sending you and Daniel Stern on the northern endurance refresher course. That would have taken the wind out of you. Well, for a few days.'

Gods, that 'optional' course was still a gap on my training record; one I wasn't keen on filling any time soon.

'He's on his way there, but not you. Something's come up – an overseas mission – and you're a perfect fit for it. And it'll keep you out of our hair for a bit.'

'Huh.'

'Cut along and see Conradus for the details, but let me warn you, don't get smart. Be grateful this mission came up.'

He tapped on his keyboard, printed out an admin allocation request, and handed it to me. Then he returned to his files.

Outside Conrad's door I dithered, summoning up the courage to knock on the polished dark wood. I took a good breath and did it.

'Come.'

He looked up and stared at me for a full minute. The natural daylight was sinking fast and the low sunlight reflected in his hazel eyes, making them look like agates. I didn't have a clue what he was thinking.

'Sit down,' he said in a terse voice. He picked the file on the top of his in tray and flipped it open. He looked up at me. 'Has the adjutant given you any details?'

'No, he just mentioned it was overseas.'

He touched his screen, swivelled it round so I could read it. His hand brushed mine. We both looked down, but the moment passed too quickly.

'Conrad, I'm so sorry,' I said in a low voice. 'Not for the climb,' I added in a firmer tone. 'But I didn't think there would be any effect on the unit.'

'No, you didn't think.'

'I can only repeat that I'm sorry.'

He didn't say anything, but looked at me, his eyes more liquid and face less tense.

'I wasn't angry just for the unit and you know that.'

'Yes.' What else could I say?

'I can't run a unit efficiently when two of the most promising juniors can't exercise some self-control. I think it would be calming for us if you were away for a bit. Then we can review your future here.'

Oh, Juno, he really was thinking of throwing me out. My stomach spasmed. Maybe he would say more when we got home. I loved this man and I knew he loved me. He was able to split work and the personal sides of his life. I found it near impossible.

'Have you read the mission parameters?' He tapped the edge of the screen. I scanned the ten lines, not really taking them in. I looked over at him.

'République Québecoise?' I said. What in Hades was going on in Quebec? Pleasant, old fashioned and full of polite French speakers.

'Country in the Americas, east of Canada, north of the Eastern United States.'

'Don't be sarcastic,' I retorted.

He raised an eyebrow.

'Sorry,' I mumbled. This was the trouble working with your civil spouse who outranked you by several steps. Outside, it was the other way around.

'Read this.' He pushed the file across his desk.

The file cover was marked with a diagonal red stripe with 'CELATA' across the top. Not a red ultra file which I'd never seen and wasn't cleared to see, but the next category down. I took it gingerly and opened it with respect. I read it through, then reread the major points.

'What's the timescale on this?'

'Active now.'

I glanced at him.

'There's no possibility I have to cross the border into the EUS?' I tried not to sound as nervous as I felt.

'No, not unless the subject does a runner. But she thinks she's safe. However, Flavius will go with you and he can take over if she, and it, goes south.'

I rubbed the margin of the file sheet between my thumb and index finger.

'I presume you've been north? As a child?' Conrad said.

'We went to Toronto in Canada once to go to Niagara Falls. Dad said it was better from that side. But apart from that we mostly went to Quebec for holidays.' I half closed my eyes. 'I remember the old stone houses and the wooden clapperboard cottages. Sometimes we went to Montreal and I remember swimming in the Lac Saint-Pierre.'

'Bit cold, wasn't it?'

'Freezing, but good.'

'Did you go as an adult while you were living in New York?'

'Are you kidding? I had no spare money to travel.'

The best I'd been able to manage was a vacation rental with four friends one year in Montana. My dad had died when I was twelve and I'd been uprooted from our house in New Hampshire to the open plains of Nebraska to live on an isolated farm with my joyless cousins. The day after graduating high school, I took the bus to New York and worked in various offices for peanuts until, at just shy of my twenty-fifth birthday, I'd fled to Roma Nova where my mother had been born. That was over four years ago.

I pointed at the file. 'So what's this Vibiana done that's so bad?'

'Need to know, and you don't. Just bring her back.'

3

I rubbed the plane window. Nothing but cloud. And not the pretty fluffy sort like cotton balls that made you want to jump out of the plane and bounce around on them. Just grey and formless.

'Cheer up, Bruna,' Flavius said. My friend from my first days in the Praetorian Guard Special Forces and before, he always used my nickname when we were away from formal situations. At least I had dyed light brown hair to match the name now. 'This must be better than the winter endurance exercise you could have been sent on.'

'It's still covered in snow down there.'

'What's the problem about a bit of snow? You were brought up in New Hampshire as a child. It's the same latitude.'

'I suppose so.'

I was thinking of the quick kiss on the cheek Conrad had given me when I left the house with my backpack. No arms around me, just a hand on my shoulder and a nod. At least Nonna had been warmer. As I'd unpeeled myself from her embrace, she'd taken my hands, given me a smile, then wished me good hunting. She always gave a funny little smile when she said that.

On the flight, I'd dozed in between rehearsing my cover story as a graduate student. I'd never been to university, so I prayed I wouldn't make any foul-ups. Now my ears were popping as we started the descent.

I nudged Flavius as the flight attendant came into earshot. Even over the engine noise, she'd hear us. We were speaking English to get into character, but although French was the default on this Paris-Leclerc to Montreal flight, I was sure they would understand anything we said.

'*Des déchets?*' She gave us a smile.

We dutifully put our plastic trays into the bin bag and she passed on, smile still affixed to her face.

In the enormous immigration hall at the Aéroport Louis-Napoléon, we wound our way through the snake of barriers. I yawned and looked around as we waited. My eyes prickled and I couldn't wait to get into the fresh air. I was frankly envious of the first-class passengers, elegant, understated and radiating wealth with designer clothes and uber-confident air. Looking fresh from a good night's sleep in the cabins, they were ushered through in a separate line.

Eventually the plebs line reached the barrier and I breezed through on my fake EUS passport as Lauren Jackson, but Flavius took a few more minutes on his equally fake British one as Mark Lombardi. We had Roma Novan diplomatic passports sewn into our jackets which were only to be used in extreme circumstances. Our bags came up on the carousel and as I pulled mine off I spotted the exit signs.

'Let's grab a taxi and get to our rooms.'

'We should go on the rail like budget travellers,' he said and rolled his eyes.

I made a face at him, but he was right. All three clerks at the transportation desk were crushingly helpful with traveller cards, maps and well-wishes. Minutes later we wheeled our bags onto a wide car. In the city, we changed onto the old-fashioned charming metro that ran on little wheels. It was too quiet for us to do anything but keep up chatter about tourist stuff.

Up on the plateau, we tramped through the snow down a street of old row houses near our last metro station. A hundred metres along, we stopped at one, climbed the five steps and knocked at one of twin doors.

'*Bonjour.* Madame Jackson?' A friendly smile from a dark-haired man.

'Hi, yes. Er, *parlez-vous anglais*? Or at least American?' I grinned.

'Sure, come in.' He looked at Flavius who smiled in a friendly, eager-to-please foreigner way.

'Oh, this is my friend, Mark Lombardi.'

We pulled our cases up steep stairs to the next storey and emerged into a spacious wood-floored apartment. The plumbing was previous century, but we'd survive.

'Thank you so much, Monsieur Lecroix.' I held out my hand and hoped he'd take the hint.

'I will leave you to settle in. Two weeks you've paid for, isn't it?'

'Yes. We're using Montreal as our base to explore the whole area. We may be away for a day or two at a time, but we'll be back well before the two weeks is up.'

We'd brought a supply of Napoleonic *louis* as well as the *livre québecois* they'd recently introduced; both were used at present. We had enough for our visit, but on the way back from the *supermarché* on the Avenue du Mont-Royal we checked out the nearest bank in case we needed more. We kept our conversation to tourist inanities, but as soon as we'd unpacked our supplies on the kitchen worktop, I put the kettle on and ran the washer. Under the cover of this noise, we worked in silence and made a thorough sweep of the whole apartment.

'Clean,' Flavius said after twenty-five minutes. He put his 'torch' back in its case. I peeled my surgical gloves off. While he'd been using an electronic detector, I'd drawn the short straw of the physical check which included poking in places nobody normal would want to touch.

'Agreed. Let's get some supper.'

He cooked some of the pasta and vegetables while I checked train times.

'We're going to have to leave at six tomorrow morning,' I told him as we finished eating.

'Early night then.' Flavius looked at me, a question in his eyes. There was only one bedroom despite all the living space.

'I'll take the floor with the cushions from the couch,' I said. He went to speak, but my new cell phone pinged with a message. *'Hi Lauren, calling round with a bottle of wine to say bienvenue to my city. With you in 2 minutes. Bisous. Francine.'*

'Supplies,' I said and grinned at him.

We crept downstairs to be ready to open the door quickly. Flavius flattened himself against the wall just beyond the door's swing. I counted to twenty. Nothing. Odd. After another minute, I sat down on the stairs. After five more minutes, I fished out my cell and messaged 'Francine', in reality a Roma Nova legation courier. No reply. *Merda.*

'Go upstairs,' I whispered to Flavius. 'The bedroom balcony looks out onto the street. See if you can see anything strange. There should be a girl with a backpack. And a bottle of wine.'

After five minutes, he crept back down. 'Nothing.'

We exchanged a glance.

'Either she's compromised or we are,' I said. 'I'm the only one in our group who knew she was coming here. And only the PGSF commander at the legation here knew from their end.' The last thing I wanted to do was to go out on a freezing dark night after a transatlantic flight in economy, but we couldn't leave her out there if the ungodly were about.

'It's been nearly fifteen minutes since you had that first message,' Flavius said as we threw on jackets, hats and scarves. I buckled on my boots and thrust some basics into my parka pockets as Flavius did the same.

I glanced at my watch. 'Eighteen now. Let's make for the metro station.' I pulled on my gloves as we left the building, stowing the keys in the inside zipped pocket. A dog-walking couple, a middle-aged woman and two teenagers were hurrying along the street. Harsh streetlights cast shadows from the first-floor balconies down onto the frost-covered sidewalk. The contrast of pitch black and white made it hard to focus enough to spot anybody who could be hiding behind the steps up to the entrance doors. We crossed to the other side and stood by a fenced off building lot. Flavius pretended to check his cell while I cast around. Nothing.

On the metro station forecourt I pushed open the weird pivoted door into the station. Flavius followed close behind. In the tiled booking hall streams of commuters flowed round a cluster of people in the centre. Through legs, I could see a man kneeling on the cold floor, next to a figure on the ground. Then I saw the pool of dark red liquid by the figure's head.

4

Flavius grabbed my arm and pulled me into one of the corridors as if heading for the down escalator. A service recess at the side. We leant back against the wall.

'Somebody would have been watching for a reaction from whoever she was meeting,' Flavius said. Saying that, he'd confirmed what I'd registered almost without seeing. It was a young woman lying on the floor. Wide padded loops projected from under her – a backpack. It had to be Francine. The reflection of red and blue flashing lights bounced off the white tiled wall. Ambulance.

'Do you think she'll made it?' I said.

He shook his head.

I turned away and clamped my lips together hard. A sour taste filled my mouth and I nearly threw up. I took some deep breaths.

'You okay?' Flav gave me a funny look.

'Sure.' I nodded. 'We have to retrieve that bag. If the paramedics or the hospital find what I think's in it and put it together with her ID, there'll be a massive diplo-fit.'

Flavius tapped furiously on his phone. 'Most likely place is the university hospital.'

'Find us a back way out of this station and let's grab a taxi.'

'I always wanted a passenger who said "follow that car".' The cab driver chuckled.

'It's an ambulance, not a car and that's my sister in it,' I snapped.

'Oh. Sorry.'

Flavius touched my forearm. I glanced at him and he shook his head.

'No, I'm sorry,' I said to the driver. 'I didn't mean to be rude. It's just that I'm worried.'

'It's okay, I understand. I'll get you there almost before they unload her.'

I closed my eyes and leant back. He raced down the main boulevard and the cab juddered as he pulled it round the corner into the street with the emergency room entrance.

Half a dozen ambulances hovered there like bees waiting to go into the hive. I thrust three five-*louis* notes at him with the moustachioed Joseph Napoleon's image staring out. Flavius was peering at his phone, then the ambulances.

'That one,' he said and pointed to the one at the back of the queue. 'I took a photo of its registration plate as we followed it.'

We waited in the freezing air as each ambulance released its contents. The second ours opened the back doors, I hurled myself at the gurney, pushing the two paramedics aside.

'Emily, oh, Emily!' I shrieked. 'Speak to me!' Then I started crying.

'Stand back please,' one said firmly. They lowered the gurney from the ambulance.

'She's my sister,' I said and grabbed the nearest paramedic's arm and shook it. They were both staring at me. I spotted a quick movement behind them, a figure reaching into the ambulance. I had to stop them turning round. I burst into sobs, my chest heaving and waved my arms around as in deep distress. They exchanged glances. One patted my shoulder.

'We understand you're upset, but the best place for her is inside. Please stand aside and let us take her in.'

Flavius was clear of the ambulance, the precious rucksack in his hand. He walked out of the entrance area, bag slung over his shoulder, and disappeared. I glanced down at the figure swathed in blankets on the gurney. She moaned, her eyes fluttered then opened. Gods, she was alive.

'Lauren?' she whispered.

'Yes, you did it.' I studied her face, it was white, but her eyes focused on mine. She even tried to move her hand.

'*Que les dieux soient loués,*' she gasped.

The paramedics pushed past me through the automatic doors and wheeled her into the hospital. I crept away and hurried back into the main street where Flavius was waiting for me. We searched up and down for a possible tail.

'Flav, she was alive. And there was a funny smell.' I stopped and it struck me what the red liquid was. 'Oh gods, it was the wine that spilt, not her blood.'

We eventually found a public payphone and I called the Roma Nova legation, leaving a coded message – seemingly about a visa application – which would get routed to the Praetorian commander.

'The first things we need to get tomorrow are new cell phones,' I said. 'Either ours are compromised, there's a leak in Quebec, or worse, at home.'

'We'll be going dark. Home won't be able to track us.' Flavius frowned.

'That may not be the worst idea in the world.'

With that cheerful thought, we walked back to the row house and our beds.

We left our original cell phones in the apartment. If they were compromised, then the opposition knew already where we were. But we took our portable scanners, IDs, documentation and ready cash with us in the backpack 'Francine' had delivered to her cost.

A change of clothes made us look a little more respectable and we reversed our jackets. I plaited my hair and bound it on top of my head, pushing it under my hat. Not marvellous, but it would have to do.

In the Rue Sainte-Cathérine we had a choice of phone stores. The relief of being connected again was immense. We had two hours to spare so we found a coffee shop and spent time setting our phones up.

'Are you okay, Bruna? You've gone quiet.'

'I guess.'

'Look, it could be worse,' Flavius said. '"Francine", or whatever her name is, is in the hospital and you've alerted the legation. They'll send somebody round this morning to check on her, if they didn't last night. Thanks to your hysterical sobbing act, we've retrieved the backpack from the ambulance. And we didn't get raided last night by the ungodly.'

The locks in the apartment wouldn't have stopped a teenage burglar but Flavius had set wire alarms everywhere as well as IR beams.

'I suppose "Francine" could actually have had a genuine accident and we're overreacting...'

'Tell me you don't really believe that!' He rolled his eyes.

'No, but I have the feeling there's more to this than the simple retrieval of a wayward government scientist.'

'Something political?'

'It usually is, whatever anybody says,' I replied. The PGSF's sole reason for existing was to be the intelligence and covert operations unit of the force that protected the imperatrix and state of Roma Nova. I'd known that much even before I'd started serving in it. Conrad had said nothing. He'd just given us the task. It was our duty to carry it out. But still...

I glanced at my watch. 'Let's get to the university.'

'You've got the syringes?'

I nodded. 'Let's go get her.'

The university, mostly glass and steel buildings from the late 1990s, huddled near the base of the Mont-Royal, the hill that gave the city its name. We'd booked tickets for a public lecture that let us into the main building. Over a hundred people filled the room and I couldn't see anybody watching us as we snuck out one at a time.

I checked the campus map on my phone while I waited for Flavius. The door from the lecture hall opened. I knelt down as if tying the lace of my sneaker, but as soon as I saw his face, stood up.

'Through into the next building, then the cafeteria. The library's the building after that.' I pointed at a pair of glass double doors.

'Sure you can get into the library?'

'Gods, I hope so,' I replied. 'The adjutant assured me the student pass was universal and the chip with my fake student history is supposed to be bombproof.'

'Ha! Shouldn't come to that.' He bent over, gave me a quick kiss on the cheek. 'I'll go and collect the hire car and see you in an hour or so. I'll be by the library west entrance.'

I nodded, slung the backpack across one shoulder and pushed the right glass door open.

'Well, it's unusual to subscribe a student before they've started their research programme, but your supervisor's letter explains everything.' Nothing was out of place about the librarian from her vowels to her navy twinset and thin-framed spectacles under a head of well-disciplined hair.

'Thank you so much.' I gave her my friendliest smile. 'I just want to get ahead with the reading. Which section deals with the scientific application of precious metals?'

I picked all the volumes on silver mining and processing in central Europe; one was even titled *Roman Silver Mining and Processing in the Ancient and Modern Worlds*. I waited for them to be delivered and sat with my notebook at one of the few empty desks in line of sight of the librarian's desk. The red-brick interior of the library was quaint but matched the style of the building exterior. It was one of the few older buildings I'd seen in the mass of glass and concrete blocks.

My five books arrived and I checked my watch again. According to my briefing, our target's library check-in records showed she came here every day in the early afternoon and stayed for two to three hours. I had no idea how home had hacked into a foreign university's records, but I was sure their output would be accurate. Anyhow, I'd hijacked all the books I thought she might want.

After an hour of reading that was so boring it threatened to put me off the silver industry forever, a sturdily built woman about mid-thirties, dark brown, almost black, hair checked in at the librarian's desk. She was carrying a crimson coat and leather briefcase and wore boots with red piping . I kept my head down but watched her through my eyelashes. I couldn't hear her words, but her voice wasn't English. More than that, she fit the description. She talked in an animated fashion, as if she was frustrated. The librarian nodded in my direction. The woman spun round and marched over toward me. Gods, she looked pissed with something!

'Excuse me, but I need that book urgently.' She jabbed her finger at my desk. The one on Roman silver mining.

'Well, I'm sorry,' I replied in English, attempting to sound sincere. 'I'm reading it at present and using it to make notes. I'll make sure I finish with it this afternoon. You can reserve it for tomorrow.'

'No, I need it today.'

'Then you're going to be disappointed.' I went back to my studying.

She stood there, silent, but the anger and frustration rolled off her. Her hand darted out in the direction of the book, but I was faster and clamped her wrist. I stared up at her.

'What do you think you're doing?' I said.

'I must have that book!'

'Really? And who are you to insist?' I held my breath. Would she answer?

'I'm a visiting professor from Europe and I have a class to prepare.' A pink tinge grew in her face and she glanced down. Not a very good liar.

'Then you know the rules of academic libraries. What's your name?'

'Why do you want to know?'

'You could just be another student being obnoxious. You can get lost.'

She hesitated, looked at my notes, the books, then back at me.

'I'm… I'm Doctor Vibiana from the Central University in Roma Nova. Now hand over that book.'

Juno, she'd used her real name. But she thought she was dealing with some normal EUS student, not a Praetorian hunting her.

The librarian was looking in our direction and not in a positive way. My opportunity. I bent down and grabbed my bag, abandoning my notepad and pencil, and took Vibiana's arm.

'Let's take this outside, we're disturbing the other students.'

Vibiana clamped her lips together, but she gave a quick nod, picked up her bag and coat. I mimed 'sorry' to the librarian as we passed her desk. In the entrance lobby, I steered Vibiana towards a side bench.

'Now look, this is a ridiculous quarrel. Actually, I have something that if you're interested in the scientific application of silver you might find very useful.'

'What?'

I fished in my backpack, shucked off the packet, brought out the preloaded syringe and stabbed her in the upper arm through her jumper. Her eyes widened. She made a token struggle, then slumped. I caught her and eased her down onto the bench. I glanced left and right. A man hurried round the corner and looked at us. I made a drinking gesture and rolled my eyes. He grinned back. As soon as he'd disappeared, I secured my bag and hers, then dragged Vibiana up, pulled her arm across my shoulders and grabbed her coat. Right now I needed a third hand and arm, but it wouldn't be for more than a few minutes. We lumbered on into the next corridor. She wasn't completely out of it, just sedated. Her legs and feet cooperated most of the time.

The door leading to the service basement was halfway along the corridor. I glanced left and right. Nobody. I propped Vibiana against the wall. Once my scanner had revealed the door keypad code, I pushed it open and heaved Vibiana through into a world of concrete, cabling and everlasting conduit. Thank the gods, the stairs down had a solid tubular rail. Luckily, the exit door to the street was only a few metres away. Propping Vibiana's drooping form against the boiler cage, I yanked the door bar down and opened it a few centimetres.

No sign of Flavius or a car.

Crap.

A moan. I looked back at Vibiana. She was shaking her head and struggling to stand up. No. I pulled the second syringe out of my bag, shucked off the cover and grabbed her arm. She opened her eyes.

'You.' She looked at my hand. 'Wass that?'

I said nothing but yanked her arm and jabbed the syringe in the flesh. She gasped, then slumped back. Sometimes I hated the things I had to do. She must have done something really bad for Roma Nova to have sent a snatch team. She looked harmless enough to me.

I looked out again. No car. Vibiana would start stirring again in another ten minutes.

'Flav, where the hell *are* you?' I hissed into the phone. The voicemail cut in. I nearly threw it on the floor, but shoved it in my pocket instead. A clang in another part of the basement. Footsteps in the distance but getting louder.

Hades.

I went back to Vibiana, eased her up and dragged her towards the outside door. I pushed the bar down, then grasped her by the arm and pulled her through. A blast of cold air hit us. I pulled the door shut and shifted away from it. At least we were at the back of the building, but it was still too open. All we needed was some nosy student or worse, one of the campus security guards to see us and it would all go in the crapper. I stood in front of Vibiana and searched around again, staring at any car that drove past. There were only a few, but my heart leapt as each one approached. The disappointment was immense when I saw none of them was driven by Flavius.

Vibiana murmured, 'Wass goin' on?' I spun round. She was moving her head, but was struggling to prise her body off the stone wall. I had two to three minutes before she started shrieking for help.

5

A screech of tyres behind me.

'Bruna. Here.'

Flavius. Oh, thank the gods. I nearly sobbed.

We bundled Vibiana into the trunk, threw her coat over her, stowed her bag and leapt into the car.

'Where the hell have you been?' I shouted at him.

'Some arse-ache of a security guard held me up as I didn't have a pass for the car. I had to go through a rigmarole explaining I was picking up a friend who'd hurt her foot and couldn't walk. Make sure you limp if we get stopped.'

We drove out of town into the boondocks; mostly flat and empty with the odd farm building, but after the first settlement Flavius turned left into a wooded area. The tarmac ran out and became a dirt road, the puddles filled with ice. According to the digital map, it dwindled into a track.

Flavius cut the engine and we got out, slamming the doors. A shout came from the trunk. We exchanged glances.

'Ready?'

I nodded. He was strong and I was agile, but there must have been over a hundred and ninety pounds of angry woman about to come at us. I released the catch and the lid swung up.

She struggled up and took a deep breath, coughing in the cold air. She swung her legs over the rim and with some difficulty rolled herself out of the trunk. Then she launched herself at us.

'Who are you? What do you want?' She shook her fist in my face. I grabbed it and pushed it down.

'Marcia Vibiana.' I reverted to Latin. 'I am Lieutenant Carina Mitela, Praetorian Guard Special Forces.' I waved my gold eagle ID in her face. 'This is Optio Marcus Flavius. You are under arrest for treason under the provisions of Table Eight. You will surrender to the court and return to Roma Nova with us.'

'Apollo's balls to you. I haven't done anything wrong. Show me your evidence.'

'We are the arresting officers. The court will examine and decide on the evidence. You will surrender to us and accompany us on the first flight home.'

'And if I don't?'

I looked at her with a steady gaze. 'You *will* be on that flight, I assure you.'

She glanced at both sides of the road but we each took a step sideways to prevent any attempt at escape.

'You can't just walk into the Free Republic of Quebec and drag me off,' she protested. 'That's kidnapping.'

'Well, this is the quick way.' Gods, she was going to be awkward. I took a deep breath. 'Under the treaty provisions with Quebec, and Louisiane for that matter, we have accelerated extradition. Optio Flavius here and I can make a citizen's arrest, take you to the central police commissariat and have you detained.' Vibiana glanced from me to Flavius as if looking for a different answer. Flavius just frowned at her. 'The legation will get an extradition order to the *procureur de la république* within days and we'll be back to fetch you,' I continued. 'But you'll have all the embarrassment of a public hearing, media reporting and up to two weeks in a remand prison and still end up back in Roma Nova.' I waved my hand at her. 'Your choice.'

She scuffed her boot on the frozen ground and looked down. She said nothing for a minute.

'Why couldn't you just come and talk to me about this instead of abducting me and treating me like an animal?'

'Given your behaviour in the library and your file describing you as hot-tempered and stubborn, how could I think you would have been reasonable?' I said.

She shrugged.

Flavius took her arm and led her to the passenger side door. We had purposefully picked a car with only front doors. 'Now, you can give us your word you will sit quietly in the back and make no attempt to attract attention or attack us, or you can travel in the boot,' he said. 'Up to you. First sign of trouble and you're in the boot. Understand?'

'You Praetorians are supposed to be right bastards and it's true.'

I laughed. 'We're being pussycats with you. Now get in the damned car.'

Back in Montreal, we accompanied Vibiana to her apartment near the university and supervised her packing her things. She only had a suitcase and carry-on. We confiscated her passport.

'You don't know why I'm here, do you?' she said as we travelled through the sleet across town.

'As far as we're concerned, you're a traitor who absconded with state secrets concerning the silver trade.'

She laughed, then went back to whining about Praetorians, citizens' rights and abuse of power.

Quebec City might have been the oldest European settlement in North America but Montreal as the bigger and more important city hosted our legation. I could only be relieved as we drove up to its gates on a secluded street off Boulevard de Maisonneuve. At least we wouldn't have to listen to Vibiana yammering on for much longer. I spoke our names into the security panel and stared at it while it scanned my face. The gate slid open and Flavius drove in. We let a now sullen Vibiana out of the back of the car and escorted her through the glass doors into the red-brick building.

'We're only a small legation here, Lieutenant.' The Praetorian commander looked over her spectacles.

'I know, ma'am, but it'll only be for twenty-four hours max, just until we get the flights confirmed.'

'Yes, that's what your colleagues at home said. We've made the secure room as comfortable as possible and there'll be a guard on the door at all times.'

'She'll complain, whatever you do,' Flavius said.

'One of those, is she?'

We exchanged smiles.

'How's "Francine"?' I asked. 'The courier?'

The commander smiled. 'Not her real name, of course. She's recovering well. Sore head and a bit of concussion. She was more worried that you'd got the field pack, but she thought you'd taken it.'

'Courageous girl. But I'd like to ask her how she managed to be lying on the metro ticket hall floor.'

'We took a statement from her, once she was *compos mentis*.' She left her desk, went over to her filing cabinet and pulled out a beige folder with a broad red stripe across the front.

'Here.' She handed us a sheet. 'I hope you won't mind reading the hard copy. I don't want to message anybody outside this building with this.'

I studied her face, but the expression was neutral, so I studied the sheet instead. After the preliminaries, it ran:

After texting agents with coded message that I was in the vicinity, I pocketed my phone, then stepped towards the exit. Somebody pushed me hard on the front of my right shoulder and I fell back over something against my lower leg, presumably an object or another person's leg. I remember hearing the crash of the bottle of wine I was carrying.

I blacked out, then my head hurt abominably and my vision was blurred. Everything seemed to spin in front of me. I was loaded into an ambulance. At the hospital, one of the agents spoke to me. She said she had the field bag. The next thing I remember was lying in a hospital room.

I think it was a man who pushed me, possibly a tall woman. It was so quick. Like everybody else, he was muffled in a heavy coat and hat. This only came to me afterwards, but I think he wore sunglasses, which was odd at that time of night.

I laid the sheet down.

'Odd is a good word,' I said.

'But who was it and how did he, possibly they, know "Francine" was delivering the bag to us?' Flavius asked. 'Have you used her before?'

'First time she's done this.' The commander looked from Flavius to me. 'She's an admin clerk and volunteered. She's a mouse, hardly ever goes outside, except for shopping or some socialising, so she was quite excited.'

'Poor kid,' Flavius said.

'Well, in case our phones were hacked, we've purchased new ones, but we'll use the scrambler unit at all times.' I gave the commander a steady look. 'I hope you'll forgive us if we keep these numbers to ourselves. Francine's delivery to us was only known to you, me and our liaison officer at home.'

Her face tightened and her eyes became cold.

'I'm not accusing anybody, Captain. I think it's a hack, but let's keep to extreme operational security.' I stood. 'We're going back to our apartment to clear up. Is there a back way out of the legation?'

'Bloody hell! I thought the Praetorian commander was going to incinerate you on the spot when you said that about the phones.'

'Yeah, but it's true.'

We left the hire car at the legation and caught the metro back. It was snowing again as we trudged back along the street to our apartment. I'd be glad to get to my bed. But first we had to check whether we'd had any 'visitors'. We set our phones to silent.

'Front or rear entrance?' Flavius asked.

'You do the front.' I made for the pathway that led between the tiny gardens at the back of the row houses. The fronts may have been brick or stone but the backs were mainly clapboard with balconies jutting out. People here had built in a communal way, each garden facing inwards almost forming an elongated courtyard with the others. Not that any courtyard life was happening on this cold, snowy evening.

Each property had its own garden gate giving out onto this pathway. I checked ours hadn't been tampered with, but was surprised to find it unlocked. No bolt either. I sighed. Another sign of trust in this crushingly pleasant country, maybe.

I closed the gate carefully, making no noise as I did it. Downstairs, light seeped out of the part-louvred metal shutters, but upstairs was dark. I crept up the wooden steps to the balcony of our apartment, taking care not to slip on the ice formed in the grain of the wood. I slid into the shadow at the side, out of the sight line of the door or shuttered window. As far as I could see in the dim light, there were no tracks of any footsteps on the exposed part of the balcony.

I tapped in *'Clear to back balcony door. You?'* and sent it.

No reply. I shivered despite the thick padded coat. It must have been minus ten degrees by now. C'mon, Flav. A light on my phone. *'In and clear.'* I had the key in the back door as fast as my nearly numb fingers could manage. The balcony led into the kitchen. I'd closed the door shutter and was about to go grab the kettle to make a hot drink when Flavius held his hand up.

Visitors, he signalled with his fingers.

I touched my ear, then raised my eyebrows. He shrugged. Damn, we'd have to sweep the whole freaking apartment again. But in the meantime, we'd have to act innocent, so I made coffee as we chatted about the weather. As I ran the scanner through the rooms, I saw tiny giveaways of the visitors; magazines not quite in the same place, our sticky-tack on the doorjamb distorted, marks in the dust, the lid of the toilet cistern slightly off centre. They'd been reasonably thorough, but not careful. Not a sign of a bug, which was strange. We carried on as if we were surrounded by them.

I sipped my coffee and chatted about supper while Flavius got to work ostensibly confirming flights for three. Not even the legation here knew that we would be heading for a private airfield where the smallest transport of the Imperial Roma Novan Air Force would land tomorrow evening. No way were we risking a standard commercial flight with Vibiana. Conrad had arranged this directly with some sky jockey friend.

I bent down to the freezer and pulled a pizza out of the middle drawer along with a plastic bundle of bubble wrap. Inside was a freezer baggie with my Glock. At the back of the next compartment, the ammunition clips. It was a compact but deadly 177 mm of firepower.

Flavius looked up as I unwrapped it. His eyebrow shot up. I laid my fingers to my lips. In the bathroom, I ran the shower, wrapped my hands in the thickest towel in the bathroom but left some wriggle room and checked the movement of the little weapon. Stuffing it in my pocket, I reached up and stopped the shower.

Flavius handed me a note.

Didn't know we had authority for arms.

I scribbled back, *We don't, but hey.*

He made a face and rolled his eyes. I just grinned.

Via the courier?

That's why we had to recover the bag.

We ate, washed up and went for an early night. I lay under the blankets with the scrambler attached to my new phone and texted Conrad the number.

The reply zoomed back immediately.

'Why the change? Problem?'

'Precaution. Unfriends at work. Tell you when we land.'

'Now.'

I gave him the short version.

6

'What in Pluto do you mean, "she's gone"?' My heart pounded and I felt the heat of my temper rising.

The legation Praetorian commander's face was pink. Anger? Embarrassment? I didn't care.

'Look, Captain,' Flavius said in a voice trying to be reasonable, 'this is a massive breach.'

'Of course it is,' she snapped. 'I don't need an *optio* to tell me that.'

'Tell us exactly what happened, ma'am,' he said.

She flopped into her chair behind her desk and waved us to two in front. I just stood there, arms tight across my chest, trying to keep my anger in.

Flavius looked steadily at me. I shrugged then plunked myself in one of the chairs.

'We put her and her luggage into the secure room and checked her every hour,' the commander said. 'There is no window, no exit apart from the door where a guard was stationed all night. We gave her a bottle of water and a tray of food – only a plastic spoon.'

She gave me a look as if expecting an argument. I said nothing.

'When we collected the tray,' she continued, 'Vibiana asked to use the bathroom. She had her handbag, a plastic carrier bag with toiletries, and the towel we'd supplied. The guard reports hearing some musical humming, then water noises – the lavatory and the shower. After a while, she noticed the shower was still running, so she knocked on the door. No answer. She knocked again. When there was still no answer, she went in and found the bathroom empty.' She looked down at her desk.

'Window?' I said.

'Yes,' she replied in a low voice.

'Show us.'

It was depressing. The bathroom was a short way along the basement corridor, next to the exercise room and used by legation staff sweaty from their fitness efforts. It must have been converted as the frosted window was a standard size. And as a non-secure room, it had no bars nor an alarm.

'It's in the basement with a high railing and mesh cover over it.'

'Yes, but that's designed to keep others out,' I said as I leaned out of the open window. The release catches on the inside were now open. The service alleyway it gave onto was closed off by a metal gate at the end with a one-way security lock. I took a deep breath of the chill air, then pulled myself back into the bathroom. 'What time did the guard notice the shower was still running?'

'Just after ten yesterday evening. We tried to call you, but had no reply. We sent a flash signal home, then I sent out a search party, but they found nothing.'

'Show me her things.'

In the secure room, Flavius and I searched through Vibiana's suitcase and carry-on, but found only the usual stuff. Her briefcase was down the side of the table. I opened it and picked through the folders, but nothing sprang out. They were mainly academic extracts, some notes, a printout of a geological report and a list of books from the library. One title was underlined. The one I had taken out on Roman silver mining that Vibiana wanted so badly. Was that so significant?

'No coat or boots,' said Flavius. 'Did she actually go to the bathroom dressed for outdoors?' He tried to keep the irritable tone out of his voice, but failed.

'Look, we're a legation guard, not intelligence people like you. We don't suspect every action, word or breath. We're not that paranoid.' Flavius stepped on my foot before I could retort. 'Vibiana complained about being cold,' the commander continued. 'So we didn't think it unusual she kept her coat on.'

The three of us stood there for a few moments, resentful and annoyed with each other.

'Okay, let's move on,' I said after a few moments. 'Can your people check with the railroad and bus stations, and the airport, to see if they have any CCTV?' She nodded and hurried off.

'Hell's teeth,' Flavius said. 'What is it with these regulars? How hard is it to keep hold of somebody for twelve hours? Shit.' He glanced at me. 'Hadn't we better get out there, searching?'

'You go look round at the back of the building and see if you can see anything in the alleyway and check the precise timings.' I looked at my watch; only just after nine. 'I'm going back to the university library. Vibiana underlined that book on the list for some reason.'

I smiled my most saccharine smile at the librarian and explained that the woman arguing with me had felt faint so I'd called a taxi for her and made sure she got back to her room. I apologised for leaving my books out and wondered if I could have them back for half an hour.

'*Très bien*, but make sure you return them properly this time.' She didn't quite peer over her glasses like my grandmother did, but she gave me that look.

I let the one on Roman silver mining fall open naturally, but it didn't do that classic thing that happened in the movies where the book parted helpfully at the significant page.

I flicked through, but then something caught my eye. Somebody had turned a corner over. Sacrilege in an academic library. But it was the only occurrence in the whole book. I searched the page, but there was nothing interesting, just a boring description of extraction methods, angles of tools used and daily ore counts. No dots, dashes or other marks under the words to show a hidden message. That would have been childish, and surely even Vibiana hadn't been that obvious?

What *had* Vibiana done that was so secret even Conrad wouldn't tell me?

I hurried over to the photocopier, wrote my fake name of Lauren Jackson on the log sheet and found that Vibiana had copied this and three other pages. I did the same.

———

'Anything?' Flavius asked back at the legation.

'Zilch. If you don't count the four pages out of some history book she photocopied.' I handed him the pages and plunked myself on the chair in the secure room.

'Well, I've found something in her luggage that may help.'

'What?'

He unfolded a handkerchief, a beautiful thing. Delicate strands chased each other into expanding networks, all tenuously held together with tiny knots. Here and there, tiny pieces of silk interlaced with silver threads completed the random squared pattern. It was unlike the symmetrical machine-produced handkerchiefs. My cousin, Silvia, who collected these things, would kill to add this one. You would never blow your nose on it.

Flavius smiled to himself as he flattened it out on the table by the photocopied sheets. I stared at the random gaps not covered by the silk patches.

Juno.

'It's a bloody grille,' I snatched the last photocopy and draped the handkerchief over the text. The copies were the same size as the originals, thank the gods. Individual letters showed through the gaps. I looked up at Flavius. 'See if the legation has a decent cryptographer.'

'Well, ma'am, you're right, it's a grille, a turning grille based on the Cardano.' He leant back and smirked. 'I haven't seen anything this old and primitive since I did my first course.' His name was Granius and he looked as if he had as smart a mouth on him as his ancient namesake.

'Okay, I know the general principle, gaps in text revealing a message and so on, but what's this turning thing?'

'A cipher message shouldn't appear to be a cipher and the original Cardano grille did that. That was its main protection. But once the opposition gets hold of the grille, they can easily recover the text. So later cryptographers did all kinds of clever things to hinder anybody else reading the cipher apart from the grille holders including turning in 90 degrees, 180, whatever.'

'Yes, but can you bust it?'

'No problem.' He bent his head over the sheets and started scribbling notes.

Flavius and I were drinking coffee in the tiny mess bar when Granius sauntered in barely an hour later.

'This was so simple it was almost laughable.' The young cryptographer grinned. A bit too cocky, I thought, but he seemed to know his stuff.

'Okay, sit down and show us, smart-ass.' He chuckled. He set his laptop down on the coffee table, then spread the sheets and his notes out.

'The content seems to be information and instructions for different situations. These must have been a series of presets and the recipient was probably signalled by a phone text or voicemail which one to use and which book and page. The third one is probably the most relevant at this moment.' He glanced at me and handed over the first two of his plaintext notes.

The first ran, *Confirm your arrival.* And the second, *Essential you hand over now. Proceed to point 49.*

'And the third one,' I said, stretching my hand out.

Hunters still loose. Fallback point 63.

'Presumably that's us.' I glanced at Flavius. 'And where the hell is "point 63"?'

'What's the fourth one say?' Flavius chipped in. 'It must be the one she was trying to get when Lieutenant Mitela wouldn't let her have the book.'

Confirm handover.

'So she hasn't given whoever it is whatever it was she fled with. I guess that's something.'

'Or she might have but hasn't been able to confirm it.'

I stood up and rubbed the back of my neck. Our target turned out to be trained for covert operations. She had disappeared. We didn't have a clue what she was up to. Worse, who was giving her instructions? And who had searched our apartment and attempted to intercept our courier?

7

'If I may make a suggestion, ma'am?'

'Sure, Granius. All ideas welcome.'

He loaded the map program and zoomed down on the university campus.

'Point 49. If you reduce it to simple numbers four and nine that's *quattuor novem*. Well, the university library is situated in the Rue du Quartier Neuf. Seems a bit of a coincidence, doesn't it?'

'Okay, what do you suggest for point 63? That's *sex tres.*'

He tapped away for a few moments.

'I've looked on Interpedia as well. There's a Sixtrees Street in the Autonomous City of New York. Nothing else comes near it anywhere else. There's a private business library at number thirty-eight and a hotel at twenty-six.'

New York. Inside the Eastern United States. Where there was still a subpoena out on me from when I fled from the EUS over four years ago. Conrad had said there was no risk of me having to cross the border. Pluto in Tartarus. I took a deep breath to counter the fluttering in my stomach. Granius glanced at me, then when I said nothing, picked up his laptop and notes. I just about remembered to add my thanks as Flavius dismissed him.

'That's a cute idea but also crazy,' I said. 'Vibiana can't travel – her passport is locked in the legation safe. And she can't have developed into a Grade A safecracker overnight.'

We checked, much to the legation *quaestor*'s disgruntlement. He'd just sat down to his lunch. But the purple pasteboard document with the gold eagle was still in the safe.

'Now what?' I glanced from Flavius to the Praetorian commander. We sat in her office, swallowing our disappointment.

'I've emailed her photo and description to my contact in the border police to keep an eye out for her. On a strictly unofficial basis, naturally. We have no jurisdiction here and I'm sure you don't want your mission to become public. But he owes me one.' And she smiled.

All we could do was wait. I had Granius write up a report about the cypher handkerchief and his findings. We were back in the mess bar, when a breathless young Praetorian guard asked us to come stat to the commander's office.

'We've found her.' The commander swivelled her screen round. Vibiana had bound up her hair, but we recognised her dumpy figure instantly from the CCTV feed as she went through the Aéroport Louis-Napoléon. She cleared security super smoothly and arrived at the gate for the New York flight just as it was called. She must have had a priority ticket as she went ahead of the rest of the passengers. How was she travelling without her passport? Who the hell was helping her?

'Obviously, I'll have to go by myself,' Flavius commented as we studied the images again.

'Why don't you go with Optio Flavius, Lieutenant?' The commander frowned at me.

'Diplomatic reasons which security prevents me going into, Captain.' I dared her to push it.

'Really?'

'Perhaps I'll take Granius with me as backup – he seems quite sharp,' Flavius intervened. I glared at him. The commander hesitated, but after a moment nodded. Out in the corridor, I looked both ways to check nobody was in earshot.

'You are joking, Flav. Granius is only a regular grunt, a signals cypher clerk, not trained for outside ops,' I protested.

'It's either him or letting somebody else into the operation.'

'My ID is a good one and the EUS isn't expecting its black sheep to return,' I bleated.

'Now *you're* joking! I'm not explaining to the boss why you got picked up and thrown in an EUS jail. Besides it would cause an almighty diplomatic and security stink.'

'So you think I'd be caught? Am I that sloppy?' I stuck my chin in the air at him.

'Don't get huffy. It's operational procedure.'

He was right, of course, but I didn't like it. The Praetorian commander persuaded the signals chief to release Granius on detachment, but gave me a stern look. She was shut out of the full loop and didn't like it one little bit. Granius would travel as himself on his diplomatic passport as if on vacation. Luckily, he'd visited the EUS for short breaks before. I gave him my sensor and explained it was fully shielded and would get through airport security.

'Just say it's a backup battery for your cell phone.'

Flavius took Vibiana's passport with him. Whatever she'd used before to get into the EUS wouldn't be safe to use when Flavius and Granius brought her out. I drove them to the airport in the rental car. Flavius sat in the back, giving Granius a Spying 101 course.

'For the gods' sakes, do not get caught or I *will* come after you,' I said. We had ten minutes in the drop-off parking lot. 'I'll bust you out and then make your lives a total misery for at least a week.'

Granius looked worried, but Flavius just smiled at me.

'We'll be back before you know it.' He grabbed his bag and strode off in the direction of the Departures.

'Give him five minutes, Granius,' I said. 'When you enter the terminal, go and sit somewhere for ten minutes, buy a magazine or go to the men's room. What I'm saying is don't go through at the same time as Flavius.'

'It's okay, ma'am. I go through the priority line as I'm on a diplomatic passport.'

'Make sure you keep to field signals protocol,' I said. 'Remember I'm Aquila Zero, Optio Flavius is Aquila One and you're Aquila Two. No real names.'

'Sure, I know that.' He gave me a superior smile. He really was a smart-ass. I just hoped he didn't get overconfident.

I drove back to the apartment in a foul mood. I was angry about losing Vibiana, frustrated I couldn't go with Flavius to retrieve her and as anxious as hell about the hidden aspects of his operation. I parked up at the far end of the street and, pulling my parka hood up, walked back on the opposite side of the road past the entrance door as if aiming for the station. Everything looked undisturbed as I went by, peeking through the fur edge of my hood. Further up, I crossed the road and walked back briskly, fished my key out of my pocket and went in.

It was warm; the heating had kicked in. I paused at the bottom of the stairs. I couldn't smell or hear anything wrong. I slipped each of the three keys between the fingers of my right hand, flicked on the light with my left and walked up. The single-strand cotton-hair thread across the stair treads halfway up was unbroken. I let my breath out slowly. At the top of the stairs I switched on the other lights and saw I was alone. A quick check in the other rooms confirmed it. I dropped the keys in the saucer at the side and grabbed the kettle.

The ping of a message roused me from my doze.

Arrived safe & sound at hotel. Hope children behaving. See you day after tomorrow. Mark xxx

Very domestic, but that mention of children meant he'd met up with Granius. I forced myself to check the fridge and find something to eat. I was about to take a first bite out of a pizza hot from the oven when a second message pinged in.

Just seen somebody I know from work in the lobby. Don't think she saw me. Will catch up with her at dinner. xxx

Thank the gods. Granius's hunch had paid off. I checked the flight schedule. They could even be back tonight.

A harsh screech. Repeated. My phone. I reached for it in the pitch darkness. Missed. A clunk on the floor. Silence. I found the switch for the bedside light, retrieved the phone and blinked at its fierce light. Four-thirty. It screamed at me again.

'Hello, *bonjour*.'

'Thank the gods. It's Granius. We've—'

'Wait one.' I grabbed the scrambler from the bedside table and plugged it in.

'Lesson one. Don't talk on an open line, Aquila Two. Remember I told you that?'

'Yes, but this is a dire emergency.'

'Okay, calm down and let me speak to Aquila One.'

'I can't. He's in hospital.'

'What?' I leapt up. 'Tell me everything.' I drew my parka across my shoulders in the chill of the early morning unheated apartment.

'We spotted her in the hotel. She was eating by herself. Fla— Aquila One sat down on the chair opposite. She looked shocked. Aquila One and the target left their table and went upstairs in the lift, second floor, according to the light over the lift. I raced up the stairs, but saw nobody in the corridor there. I walked up and down both arms. It's L-shaped. The lift is at the corner. Nothing for twenty minutes. Then two guys came out of a room with a janitor's trolley. Wrong at that time of night and one of them was making a real effort at pushing it.' His voice was trembling. He cleared his throat. 'Aquila One hadn't called or messaged me which I thought was wrong as well. There was no sign of him. I guessed it had to be him in that trolley. They looked like real toughs. I couldn't—'

'It's okay, Aquila Two. It's okay not to confront overwhelming opposition.' Oh gods, I should have been there, not this untried and jittery clerk. 'Well done for staying calm in trying circumstances. Now, what happened next?'

'I walked past them and went down the stairs to the basement and hid behind a boiler. The two men and the trolley arrived and they bumped the trolley out to the garage. I crept forward and from the gap of the open garage door I saw them open the trolley bin and lift a body out and haul it into the boot of a hatchback. Then they pushed the trolley into a corner, stripped off their coveralls and took the lift back upstairs.'

I heard him gulp. 'Keep it together, Aquila Two. And next?'

'I grabbed the car lock code with my sensor, opened the boot. It was Aquila One. He was unconscious and his face was beaten in.' His voice took on a higher note and became breathy. 'I thought he was dead! I was frightened of moving him in case I hurt him or something was broken, but I was even more frightened of those toughs coming back.'

'What did you do?'

'I picked him up over my shoulder and staggered over to our rental car and drove him to the nearest emergency room.'

'Well done, Aquila Two. What did you say there?'

'I said I'd seen some people beating him up. When they left, I put him in the car and brought him to the hospital. Then I had to say it all over again to the civil police. Gods!'

'Okay, go and get some rest. No, wait, collect your things and get on the next plane back. We're dealing with some tough nuts here and you need to be out of the way.'

'What about Aquila One?'

'Give me the name of the hospital and I'll get somebody there.'

8

I entered the Eastern United States through Washington, the easiest entry port. Maybe they were more cosmopolitan than other EUS cities because the federal government was situated there. Passport control had been easy at Sterling-Dulles Airport; I had a shiny Quebec visa that was not given out lightly. The border control officer looked almost bored as he handed me my passport back. I released my breath; I had made it into the EUS. In the transit area I picked up a hopper to New York. The cold clear sky meant the view over the Chesapeake was bright and open. A flock of wild geese wove and flowed below our graceless metal bird. I almost relaxed.

But too soon we circled over the bays around New York. As I stood in line for the Autonomous City of New York police to check my papers, I was sure they would hear my heart pounding like a jackhammer. I'd never thought about it when I lived there – it had seemed normal then – but since I'd left, I'd learned as an outsider about how paranoid they were, how jealous of their independence within the EUS. So we all had to go through another bureaucratic control.

'Why have you flown in from the République Québecoise? And via Washington, Miss Jackson?'

'It was the cheapest deal, officer.' I smiled at him. Not full teeth; they didn't like that. 'I need to look after my pennies.'

'Okay. And what were you doing in Quebec?'

I glanced around, then leaned in and said in a low voice, 'I was flying back from Europe after working there as an au pair but I went to see my boyfriend first in Montreal. My mom doesn't like him. She was suspicious and wanted me to come straight here, but I told her the Paris–Montreal was cheaper, which it was.'

'Ha!' he said. He didn't smile, but his hard neutral expression softened. I decided not to volunteer anything more. He waved me on. I grabbed my papers as he shoved them back at me, and left as fast as I could. I was sure he was staring after me but when I glanced back, he was harassing the next pour soul.

I caught the airport shuttle into the city which dropped me off in Longacre Square. Almost blinded by the flashing advertisements, I dived into the subway, bought a seven-day pass and made for my budget hotel two blocks west of Connaught Avenue. I was within five minutes' walk of my old office at Bornes & Black and over four years away from my arrest by the FBI when I'd still been Karen Brown, EUS citizen.

I napped for an hour then just before seven that evening I made my way back to Connaught Avenue to ambush Hayden Black, my old boss.

He strolled out of his glass-fronted office building as if he were on a country walk, but still covered the ground as fast as any younger man. He was English. Proper English, not one of the 1860s left-behinds. Had he changed much since I'd left? His old-fashioned sports jacket and pants made him look like a crusty old guy from a black and white movie, just as he had been before.

If he still lived in the same apartment he would head down the avenue a hundred metres, then dive into the subway. I followed him down the steps and touched his arm as he stood on the platform. He turned, an eyebrow raised and a freezing look in his eyes.

'Don't try anything, young woman. I'm not an easy mark.'

'C'mon Hayden, it's me, Karen.'

The train arriving drowned his coughing attack and I pulled him on board.

We didn't go to his apartment, but just one stop up the subway to his club. In the anonymous, almost hidden Georgian building, he ushered me through the tall mahogany doors, through a lobby and up a short flight of stairs. Opening a plain door with a brass plaque stating 'Members' Private Room' and a red/green light panel, he ushered me in and flicked a switch to show 'Occupied'. Inside were three centuries-old chairs, bookcases and books. It smelled of leather and wood. Hayden crossed the room and poured two drinks from the tray.

'Now tell me what the hell is going on.' He handed me a glass of pale amber liquid.

'First, I apologise for startling you in the subway.' He raised one eyebrow. I felt like a rookie account exec again, the warm flush rising up my neck. I took a sip of my drink. 'I'm here on a mission to rescue somebody and there's been a hitch.'

'What a strange world you live in now, Karen. No, you're Carina now, of course. How do you think I can help you? I'm far too old to leap around playing spies.'

I winced at that, but I suppose that's what I was to him.

'I just need somebody unconnected to check a friend in hospital, to see if he's okay.'

'Can't your legation do that?'

'We're in deep undercover and we'll be gone by the time they can get somebody here from Washington.' I gave him what I hoped was a winsome smile and stretched my hand out. 'You won't be in any danger, Hayden. I just want to know he's okay.'

The text message came through early next morning:

Mark Lombardi conscious. Broken rib, bruising. Reassured him you well. Estimated discharge teatime today. Regards. Hayden.

So I had less than twenty-four hours to find Vibiana, extract her, pick up Flavius and get us all out. Fabulous.

I passed via Macy's womenswear and now looked like an out-of-town manager with a conference ahead of her. I went back to the hotel where Flavius had seen Vibiana.

I enquired about 'Mark Lombardi', my co-worker, and put on my concerned colleague act. After some persuasion, the desk clerk admitted they'd had a call from the hospital and were holding his room against his credit card. Eventually, the clerk took me up to Flavius's room which we were both shocked to see had been rifled; clothes and papers everywhere.

'Omigod, what happened here?' I ran into the bathroom as if expecting to find somebody or something. Bottles, razor and brushes scattered over the basin and floor. 'His papers for the conference?' I picked up papers from the floor, sat at the plastic laminated desk and gathered them together. They weren't his real ones, just some random stuff for his cover as Mark Lombardi. Assuming a concerned expression on my face, I pretended to look through them, then turned to the clerk.

'I'll check everything's there and report back to the conference director. There are people in our industry that will do anything to steal our processing secrets, but this is terrible! I'll pack Mark's things up, shall I?'

The clerk hesitated. 'We should report this to the police.'

'Well, I have a pretty good idea who did this and I'll be taking it up with him direct. Why don't we avoid the fuss and keep it between ourselves, hm?'

He glanced at me, at the mess and back to me. I fished a fifty-dollar bill out of my purse.

'This should cover any cleaning expenses,' I said, knowing full well the cleaner would get zilch. He pocketed the bill, nodded and left.

I took a deep breath and ran my eyes round the room. The open unit had no hiding places. Flavius's carry-on was on the floor, lid gaping and empty. The laundry bag contents, such as they were, made a small pile on the floor. I gathered and folded his clothes, stowing them in his case. The toiletries and laundry followed. The papers were for show, but I slid them into the netted section in the case lid. Now my proper search would begin.

Flavius would have avoided the obvious places: toilet cistern, underside of drawer in desk unit, the room safe. Nothing in or under the bed. Nothing hanging in a bag outside the window as they were sealed. Surely he hadn't been carrying the documents on him when he was attacked?

My heart sank. Then I spotted a gap, a tiny gap, in the wooden housing shielding the lights. It ran across the wall above the desk. Hitching my shirt up, I clambered onto the desk. Taped to the inside of the panel was a slim, long plastic baggie, untouched. I ripped it off and opened it. Vibiana's Roma Novan passport, the handkerchief and photocopies, a code sensor/scrambler and a wad of dollars.

Thank Mercury!

I zipped up Flavius's case, let the wheels down, closed the room door and made my way to the elevator. A light tingle crossed my shoulders as I waited. I retreated round the corner formed by the L-shaped corridors and took a couple of deep breaths. I didn't know where that had come from but it was never wise to ignore that particular danger signal. A sound of a door closing near the lift. I risked peeking round the edge of the corner. Two heavies had just exited a room, one more sturdy than the other. I knew him instantly. Dubnus.

Merda.

I closed my eyes to try to blot out that terrible night when he'd tried to throw me off a rope bridge high in the Gemini Alps in the pitch dark. It was a training exercise. But he'd come at me intent on terminating me. It would be recorded as an 'accident'. Unluckily for him, I'd been carrying my knives in a back waist holster. His face had never been the same and he'd been busted down to plain guard. He was one of the current legate's clients, some sort of distant cousin. She was a crap patron to have let him try such a stupid thing, but she wouldn't agree to Conrad's recommendation to throw him out entirely. She'd just smirked at me the next time she'd bothered to attend the barracks. I'd refused to let Conrad take it to Imperatrix Silvia; that would have been snitching.

What the Hades was he doing here? He knew Flav was one of my Active Response Team and closest comrade-in-arms. Was he one of the heavies who had put him in the hospital?

9

I waited a long five minutes. Flavius's case I abandoned in the corner. Grasping the sensor I'd found in his room, I looked to my left and right. Nobody. After three seconds the sensor flashed green against the keycard lock and I was in.

The two men had left, but the gods knew how long they'd be out. I scanned the room. Nothing out of the ordinary. No papers on the desk. On hangers a change of shirt and a jacket, underwear and socks in the shelf unit. I searched underneath and in the jacket pockets. A carry-on with straps like a backpack yielded nothing. I crouched down and felt under the drawer in the desk unit. A flat package, no, a black baggie taped under it. Oh, for the gods' sake, I didn't think even Dubnus could be so stupid.

I removed it gently and opened it. A new EUS passport with Vibiana's photograph – so that was why she went through passport control so easily – a letter of credit on a private account at the Argentaria Prima, valid anywhere in the world, and boarding pass printouts for three people, including Vibiana, to Roma Nova for tomorrow evening's flight. I photographed everything with my cell phone and shared it to my personal digital lockbox at home, then pushed it all back in the baggie and pressed it all back under the drawer bottom.

Were Dubnus and his buddy Vibiana's guards or bodyguards?

And who was the other man? I hadn't recognised him and by now I knew most members of the home-based Guard, at least by sight.

I checked everything was back in its place and left, making sure nobody was around when I stepped into the corridor. I'd been in and out in twelve minutes. On a wild hunch, I knocked at some of the other doors in the corridor, but only got a gruff older male voice and a young American woman in reply. I grabbed the handle of Flavius's case and went down via the stairwell to the lobby. Seeing no sign of Dubnus and friend, I settled myself in a corner seat to think what to do next. The desk clerk I had bribed glanced at me once and flushed. He looked away quickly as if I were a dirty smell under his nose. Perhaps I should ask to see the hotel register, but I doubted he would even look it up on his system for me. Despite the 'cleaning' money I gave him, he may have already regretted breaking the rules.

Where in Hades was Vibiana? Not at the hotel, it seemed, and not with Dubnus. I wheeled Flavius's suitcase out of the lobby like a normal person, bumped it down the five steps and found the private business library Granius had identified six buildings down the street at number 38. It was a double-fronted Victorian, with bay windows and a recessed wood half-glazed door. I checked the case and my coat in the cloakroom in the front lobby, crossed the diagonally tiled floor and pushed through the swing doors.

The library itself was through the next set of swing doors, after the metallic arch of the scanner. But sitting on one of the padded benches at the side was Dubnus.

Crap.

He was flicking through a magazine. His buddy was standing, one hand in his pocket and the other playing with his cell phone. Thank Juno for my dyed hair. But would he still recognise me? I turned my shoulder away. Looking straight ahead and willing myself to walk at a normal pace instead of running like Hades, I went through the scanner. I released my breath and just remembered to smile at the attendant as if I had no cares in the world. I daren't look back to see if they were watching me.

Luckily, my fake Quebec graduate student pass gave me access and I signed in as Lauren Jackson. There had only been one other guest in the register fifteen minutes before me. Dr Vibiana, Central University, Roma Nova. Hades! She was using her real name. Sloppy tradecraft in the extreme. She wasn't an intelligence or security service officer, but we knew she had some competence from the way she could handle codes and her ability to deceive the legation guards and escape. This was a rookie mistake. Or was it deliberate?

I searched the whole library and couldn't find her. Only a few of the tables were occupied and there was none with papers left without their owner. So where was she? I was still searching round when I saw the sign to the bathrooms.

I closed the washroom door silently after I'd entered. Only one stall door was closed. I crouched down to check under the door. Boots with red piping. I stood, leant against the wall and waited.

After a minute, the stall door opened. The skin round her eyes was puffed up and the rims red. She wiped her eyes and sniffed. Then she saw me and took a step back.

'You must have been expecting me after your boyfriends out there beat the crap out of my colleague,' I said.

She glanced away, then back at me with a sour expression on her face.

'Much you know,' she retorted. 'They're Praetorians like you, sent to' – she made air quotes with her fingers – '*protect* me.'

'What are you talking about? Nobody else was tasked to you except Flavius and me. And only one of them belongs to the Guard and he's not my best buddy – he tried to kill me. I don't have a clue who the other one is.'

She said nothing, but scowled at me.

'We can wait here all day or until your friends out there bust in here. But I get the impression you wouldn't be happy with that.' She opened her lips to speak, then closed them. A full minute passed.

'Okay, Vibiana, I'm wasting my time here, I can tell.' I peeled myself off the wall and reached for the door handle. 'I'll leave you to it.' I took a short silent breath. Gods, would she call my bluff?

'No, wait!' she shot out her hand and caught my jacket sleeve. She stared at me for a moment, then shrugged.

'Tell me what happened after you ran away from the legation,' I said.

'I landed in that alleyway, then released the one way lock to the street. It was freezing and dark and I didn't know what to do. I was going to find a hotel somewhere. I'd gone barely five metres, when a car drew up by me. The fat one jumped out and flashed an eagle badge at me and told me to get in. When I hesitated, he pushed me in. He apologised in a passive-aggressive way but said he had been sent to make sure I completed my mission.

'I was going to complain that the other lot – you – wanted to stop me. Now they, these two, wanted to help me. Why couldn't they make up their minds? But something jarred.' She glared at me, chin forward. 'They got me out of Quebec and here to New York where I needed to be. When your colleague sat down opposite me at dinner at the hotel last night, I nearly choked. I ran back to my room and told the fat one.' She looked down. 'I thought they'd just warn him off, that they were looking after me now. I thought it was some turf war inside the Praetorians.'

'Really?' I couldn't keep the sarcasm out of my voice.

'I didn't care who got me to my rendezvous,' she shot back. 'But when they said they'd disposed of your colleague, and laughed nastily, then took my mobile phone, I knew then I'd made a horrible mistake going with them.'

'What are you doing here, Vibiana? And don't bullshit me.'

'You really don't know, do you?'

'Are we going to play twenty questions or are you going to tell me?'

'I'm an undercover investigator for the Silver Guild. Somebody's stolen the central element for a prototype for a new process. The Guild received a message saying the thieves were willing to sell it back. I'm supposed to do the deal, but the priority is finding out who stole it and fixing that particular leak.'

'And you didn't think to report the theft?'

'We've looked after our problems internally for over a thousand years. I didn't want to get either the *vigiles* or your lot involved but I was overruled. The head of the Silver Guild, Prisca Monticola, knows a senator on the intelligence oversight committee and they fixed it up through some old girls' network.' She snorted.

My grandmother headed that committee. What did she know about this?

'Anyway, the idea was to post me as the thief and send a couple of

Praetorian squaddies after me to make it look realistic. That was you and your colleague.' She rubbed the back of her neck. 'Mercury, what a mess.'

'Why have you come here to the library?'

'I told that fat one I had to get the bank account number to draw the funds to do the deal. It was coded and in a book here.'

'But you didn't have the means to decipher it, did you?'

'No,' she mumbled.

'So why did you come here?'

'I couldn't think to go anywhere else.' She looked at me, her face pale. She clamped her hands under her armpits. 'If I don't come up with the code and do the deal, they said they'll denounce me publicly as the thief and provide proof to the accusatrix's office. I'd go down for at least ten years despite the cosy little set-up Prisca Monticola had arranged through the back door.'

'But you know it's illegal to pay ransoms and this is undoubtedly what this is.'

She looked at me as if I was a total idiot and gave a short burst of laughter. 'What century are you living in? Do you think it's never happened down the years?'

'Nevertheless, it's still illegal.'

She shrugged.

I fished the lace handkerchief, the code grille, out of my handbag and held it up in the air. Her eyes widened and she shot her hand out. But I was too quick for her.

'If you want my help to get you out of this mess, you have to play it my way. I'm prepared to help you find whoever is behind the theft, but they have to be brought before the people's court at home – no covert little arrangements.'

'Aren't you the upright one?' She nearly sneered.

I grabbed her collar points and tugged hard. 'Don't get smart with me Vibiana.' She coughed and spluttered, so I released her.

'I don't have much option, do I?' She grumped and made a big production of rubbing her neck.

'Try to sound a little more grateful, why don't you?'

10

Back in the library, I stood over Vibiana as she deciphered the bank details, meeting place and time – later that afternoon. She'd washed her face and combed her hair in the bathroom and composed herself enough to give Dubnus a curt nod when she joined him and his buddy in the library vestibule. In the street, the two men hemmed Vibiana in while they hailed a cab. It was only a few blocks away so I made my way to the bank on foot by cutting through passages I'd known when I'd lived here for seven years. They'd take forever in New York's traffic.

I loitered in the banking hall, looking at leaflets about unsuitable loans and dubious investments. After a quarter of an hour they arrived. The men looked flustered; Vibiana showed her usual downturned mouth. I joined the line next to hers, my dyed hair loose to hide my face. I'd make some random enquiry of the teller if I did reach the counter. Vibiana withdrew some cash, some bonds and the rest in sight drafts. Obviously, all prearranged. The black and white features of Governor Franklin on the five-hundred-dollar bills smiled impassively as Vibiana counted them. I still felt a surge of anger at serving up money to blackmailers. She interrupted my mood when she snapped the case shut, grasped it and marched out of the banking hall with Dubnus and buddy in tow. They took another cab back to the hotel and all three disappeared into Vibiana's room.

Now I had to figure out how to pick up Flavius from the hospital at his release time. I'd be busy shadowing Vibiana at the meet to retrieve the stolen element. Flavius wouldn't know I was here in New York, what the changed plan was or anything. I couldn't risk him coming back to the hotel and trying to arrest Vibiana. Maybe I could send a cab with a message. Nah. They might miss him. With his regular features, brown hair, brown eyes and quiet manner, Flavius looked so unremarkable. Perfect for a spook, but useless now.

Of course! Hayden. He knew Flavius, knew his cover name and when he would be discharged.

Hayden was in the inevitable business lunch at Bornes Black, but I left a message with his superior assistant. From her voice, I'd bet good *solidi* she was the same near-godlike being who'd glided up and down the carpeted corridors when I'd been an account assistant there.

I called the car rental and arranged for an SUV, fully fuelled, to be delivered to kerbside outside my hotel entrance at six that evening. I'd pay them to wait for up to four hours. I winced at the quotation, but gave them my personal credit card number. The clerk insisted on seeing ID so I had to go to the office across town. As I had no driver's licence nor any document showing an EUS address in the name of Lauren Jackson, I was forced to show him my Roma Novan diplomatic passport with licence certificate and give the Washington legation as my address. Risky, but hopefully it would take a few hours for my name to come up on any watch list. We'd be gone by then, but the clock would be ticking. Then, using Flavius's scrambler, I phoned home.

'What in Hades are you doing in the EUS?'

I explained and Conrad's voice became crisper as we talked through options.

'Agreed, you couldn't do anything else,' he said. 'I don't like this business with Dubnus.' I heard tapping on a keyboard. 'He's marked as being on leave, on a research travel warrant. What in Hades is that?'

'Signed by Legate Vara?'

'Yes. Damn the woman. And don't repeat that.' However frustrated Conrad felt with his superior officer, he was intensely loyal to the Praetorian Guard and respected the command structure.

'Well somebody's been leaking info about us and our mission,' I said. 'Maybe we should make sure the FBI haven't been tipped off about me. Who's the liaison officer?'

'Leave it with me. And I'll personally prepare a different extraction RDV and get back to you within the hour. Whatever happens, Dubnus is finished. With your testimony, we'll be able to chuck him out once and for all, whatever Vara says.' He paused. 'Pluto, I hate you being in that place. Be careful.' His voice almost cracked. 'Please.'

Thank Juno, Hayden messaged me shortly afterwards and agreed to pick up Flavius from the hospital and meet me at my shabby hotel. Hayden was respectable and looked respectable. People tended to do as he asked. I was confident that Flavius would be there in good order and good time. Asclepius look out for him, though.

I grabbed a quick sandwich in the bar where I'd shared my first meal with Conrad five years ago. Nostalgia? Maybe, although it was a good memory despite our bickering then. From there, I walked until I found a thrift shop for a change of clothes. Teamed with some retro spectacles, a black faux leather backpack and a grey coat, I doubted some of my closest colleagues would recognise me as I exited the shop.

I dived into a party shop and bought a black wig. I'd pin it on later, but well before I went to observe at Vibiana's rendezvous. Not perfect, but people underestimated how good they were as a temporary disguise. Most people took no notice of others walking along the street unless they were looking for them or were suddenly stunned by their fabulous appearance.

The vehicle screech tore into my thoughts.

'You!'

A nasal tone to a shout directed at me. A blue flashing light. *Merda!* I stopped and looked around as if to find out who they were shouting at.

'You in the grey coat, stand where you are.'

I pointed at my chest and mouthed, 'Me?'

A woman, hair plastered to her skull and ending in a bun that looked glued on, jumped out of the car. Tight grey suit and tight pale face. She hadn't changed her look for five years. Special Agent O'Keefe.

Double crap.

She'd threatened me when I was still Karen Brown, average New York officer worker. If she caught me with my fake 'Lauren Jackson' passport, I was toast. Fifteen years minimum in the federal pen for espionage plus a monumental diplo-row between Roma Nova and the Eastern United States.

No way.

I swallowed hard then pasted on a smile I didn't feel.

'Yes?'

'Well, Miss Brown or should I say Mrs Mitela? Here we are again.' She smirked. My fingers itched to smack it off her face, but instead I thrust my hand in my pocket. She tensed, went for her waist holster, but I was faster. I brought out my cell phone and tapped the video app.

'Special Agent O'Keefe,' I said. 'You're looking as wonderful as ever. What can I do for you?'

She flushed. Her head tilted up. 'I'm arresting you, a known fugitive and traitor to the EUS, and taking you in for questioning relative to espionage activities.' She stretched out her arm to grab me. The man who had been driving her car came round the back and advanced towards me.

'Stop!' I shouted. Just for a moment, they hesitated. 'I am an accredited Roma Novan diplomat. You cannot search or detain me without my *nuncia*'s agreement. You may send details of your so-called charges to the legation and *they* will decide on the next steps. Right now, I'll be on my way.'

She stepped in front of me and lunged for my phone but I dodged her.

'Just because you signed some papers doesn't mean you're not a traitor,' she snapped. 'You may have gone to live in that stupid little country, but now you're back here, I'm going to put you away.'

'Really? I think you're exceeding your authority, Agent O'Keefe. I've done nothing to concern you here. I'm on a private visit. I've even stopped by to see my old boss and say hello. You can ask him if you like.' I gave her a steady look, praying she wouldn't see any of my internal fear. If she or the man actually pulled a weapon on me, I'd be sunk. 'As you can see, I'm recording this and the *nuncia* will be sending a copy to your director and to your external affairs secretary. Still Mr Hartenwyck, is it?'

She took a step towards me, thrusting her face forward so her breath warmed my skin. Peppermint. 'Don't you fuck with me, Brown – Mitela – whatever your name is. It might take me an hour or even two to get the paperwork, but you aren't going anywhere.'

'Step away from me, Agent O'Keefe. You're invading my personal space for the purpose of intimidating me. This is police harassment. I'll be filing a complaint through my legation.'

Two dark pink blotches bloomed on her face. 'I'll find you. This city has cameras everywhere. And then I'll have the pleasure of taking you down.' She stomped back to her car, snatched the door open at the same time as jerking her head at the man, signalling him to get in the car.

I stood on the sidewalk and watched them drive off. When they'd disappeared, I stumbled over to the nearest building, leant against its rough brick wall and released a long breath.

Totally forbidden when on operation, I nevertheless downed a brandy at the nearby bar. Perched on a high stool, elbows on the plastic-topped counter, I replayed the conversation with O'Keefe in my head. She couldn't get any kind of effective paperwork through the diplo channels that fast, could she? Even if the legation in Washington cooperated, which I didn't think it would. But I knew how relentlessly she and Jeffrey Renschman, the EUS enforcer, had been hunting me five years ago. He was dead now. I left some bills on the bar counter and went back to the thrift shop to change my clothes again.

Exiting the subway ten minutes before Vibiana was due to leave for her rendezvous, I ambled along, trying to look as inconspicuous as possible. There were plenty of shops full of glittering nonsense to stare into.

She marched out of the hotel glass door, her chin forward and a concentrated look on her face. Dubnus and buddy stuck close behind her. He searched around as if expecting to find somebody. Juno, had Vibiana spilled and told him about me? His gaze flickered for a moment as it touched me, then passed over me on to other women walking along.

They hailed a cab and dived in. As it lurched into the dense traffic I stripped off my coat to show my smart suit jacket underneath and waved frantically at the next cab.

'See that cab with the stupid glowing toy? Follow it.' I leapt in. 'Go!'

'Okay, lady, keep your hair on.'

I pulled the wig off and smirked at him in the mirror. He burst out laughing. 'Now I've seen it all!'

'We're heading for Little Italy, just off Mulberry Street.'

'Are you some kind of cop?'

'More of a private insurance agent.'

'Uh-huh. I guess you want me to wait, too.'

'Unless you've got somewhere else you need to be.' I fluttered a fifty-dollar bill within his peripheral sight.

He reached out and plucked it from my hand.

Vibiana's cab stopped in the narrow side street designated in the coded message. Red-brick buildings rose six storeys, making this dull day even more oppressive. I glanced at my watch. Sunset in twenty minutes. Dubnus stabbed at a bell push in a recessed entrance. The metal door opened inwards and the three disappeared inside. We parked up, miraculously finding a space on the street near an open stacked parking lot whose contents looked as if they'd spill out over the road. I plugged in my headphones as if listening to music on my phone during a boring wait, and switched on the receiver, then the recorder. The bug I'd attached under Vibiana's collar was so tiny, and well shielded. As long as she didn't take her coat off, we were good.

Silence. Surely they hadn't detected the bug. Or were they doing that staring at each other thing they did in the movies. Rustling of clothes. No, Vibiana was being searched.

'She's clean,' came a New York voice in English.

'Now to business.' A woman, older, accented voice. 'I'm sure our local colleagues will excuse us if we revert to Latin. Much easier for us.'

'Sure, but no funny business.'

'Do not be concerned – you will receive your part.' Her English was formal, not fluent, so she wasn't at home here.

'Well, Vibiana,' she reverted to Latin. 'Your guild has seen sense. You have the funds?'

'Yes.' Vibiana sounded as if she'd flunked the most important test of her life.

'Show me.'

I heard the sound of the lock clicks opening, then a thunk as the case lid hit something. A table?

More rustling, this time paper, and the thrum of somebody flicking banknotes. The case closed again.

'That all seems in order.' The older woman's voice.

'My transformer element?' Vibiana.

'Of course. I almost forgot.' Whoever she was, this older woman was enjoying herself. Well, that would stop once the voiceprint identified her.

Crackling of plastic, then silence for a minute. I thought the bug had stopped working.

'It seems intact.' Vibiana said in a sullen voice.

'Off you go, then, dear.' The older woman's voice was light, as if laughing.

'You—'

'Yes?'

'Never mind.'

Rustling noise again and a door opening. Vibiana emerged, followed by Dubnus. He crossed his arms and smirked at her.

'You can find your own way back.'

'I thought you were supposed to protect me.' She looked as cross as Hades.

'We've done our bit. Now piss off.'

'Bloody Praetorians!'

I let her stomp down the street in the slush before having the cab pull up a few metres ahead of her. As I got out I glanced back to make sure Dubnus wasn't watching, but he'd disappeared and it was unlikely he'd recognise me at this distance in the gloom.

'Get in,' I said, holding the door open for her. I hadn't understood before what a 'fulminating look' meant. Now I knew.

Back at my hotel, the rental SUV was waiting; snow was gently settling on its grey roof. I signed the paperwork and the driver trudged off down the street not having said a word more than necessary. I didn't tip him. Flavius, his bag by the side of his chair, was waiting in the small lobby. Even though the light was dim, he looked pale apart from the large bruise covering his left cheek.

'At last. I thought you'd got lost.' He smiled at me and his face transformed from the ordinary into the dazzling. He winced. 'I got them to pack your bag so we can leave straightaway.' He glanced over at Vibiana who was getting a soda and a snack bar at the machine. Flavius eased himself up, catching his breath, but waved my hand away. I handed him the keys, leant towards him and whispered.

'Get in and set the navigator to Toronto.'

'Can we cross the border now?' he said in an equally low voice.

'I haven't heard back about our new extraction point, but we need to get out of the city and that's as good a place to head to as any.'

Anxious to the point of paranoia at its entry points, the Autonomous City of New York didn't seem to care who left. After a cursory look at the passports Flavius and I showed – Vibiana was back in the trunk – we were waved through in a second. Once out of view, I released Vibiana and soon we were out on the freeway, cruising at one mile per hour less than the limit. Flavius frowned when I edged it over. He was right; we didn't want to be stopped by the cops for something as stupid as speeding. At the first rest area, I took Vibiana into the women's bathroom. I took hold of her arm, leant into her and whispered direct into her ear to strip to her underwear.

'What? You're joking. It's freezing.'

'Better freezing for a few minutes than dead,' I whispered again. 'Hurry up. We don't want any interruptions. And keep your voice down.'

'What do you mean?' She hissed at me.

'Dubnus and his buddy may have planted Mars knows how many bugs on you. Luckily, he's not a specialist so we should find them easily.'

'Mercury, will this never end?'

'Dubnus could be listening now to everything you say, or tracking us. You're supposed to be an investigator, so you must be aware of this kind of thing.'

'We don't descend to using this kind of spying gadget.' She looked down her nose at me as if I were something crawling across the floor. At least I wasn't as dirty as the floor we were standing on.

'Nevertheless, you will submit to a search.' I looked at her steadily and waited.

'Oh, very well.' She threw her coat at me.

She was clean.

Toronto was a good seven hours away, but I wasn't happy about attempting the border even if we mingled with the tourists going through near Buffalo Creek. Apart from the crossing itself, the Canadians would be watching from their observation point at Fort Erie on the other side and would send us pleasantly but firmly back to the EUS within the hour if there was the least irregularity.

We'd been on the road for an hour. Luckily, it had stopped snowing, but the falling temperature would mean ice on the road. A faint snore erupted regularly from the back from Vibiana. Flavius sat in the front passenger seat, tense, eyes closed and getting paler by the minute. I pulled over.

'What?' Flavius jerked awake.

'Nothing, it's okay.' I jumped out, pulled the rear door open and poked at Vibiana. 'Time to wake up.' She blinked, then frowned at me.

'What now?'

'Swap with Optio Flavius. He needs to lie horizontal.'

'He looks perfectly comfortable to me. I need the rest.'

'Gods, Vibiana, can't you see he's in pain? Every jolt on this freeway is like a *gladius* jab. Now get out.'

'I'm all right, Bruna, really,' Flavius said, his stiff jaw and wince on his face lying for him.

'Don't bullshit a bullshitter, Flav. In the back and lie down.'

Both were about to argue more when my cell phone pinged. Conrad had sent our exfiltration point.

11

Cumberland Field was flat, icy and deserted; three hangars for the aero club, a wide lane of passive reflective markers that winked at us in our headlights as we swept round onto the access road. I slowed down and killed the headlights. At the entrance, a lightweight padlocked chain held two chain-link gates together. Normally, Flavius and I would have climbed over, but at present he couldn't and I was pretty sure Vibiana wouldn't. I drove on fifty metres and pulled over to the edge of the road by some trees.

I checked the likely temperature. The forecast was for –1 °C lowest. We'd sit it out here. I checked the zipped section at the back of Flavius's bag. He still had his thermal blanket. I ripped off the cover and wrapped it round him, turning him gently, I thought.

'Ow, Bruna, watch it,' he yelled.

'Well, it's this or freeze.'

'Great choice.' He grunted, but let me finish. He had his coat and hat, and I tucked another blanket from the box in the trunk around him. I fetched two more for Vibiana.

'Now bundle up and stay as warm as possible.' I opened the driver's door.

'Where are you going?' Vibiana grabbed my arm, panic in her eyes.

'To make sure we can get in quickly when we need to.'

I gave Flavius the keys; I didn't trust Vibiana not to drive away and leave me stranded.

I closed the door quietly and trotted down the road. After checking both ways there were no moving lights indicating vehicles, I ran across to the airfield gates. The padlock was a standard hardware one – no real protection. I still had the set of picks Nonna had given me when I'd joined the Praetorian Guard. 'Never let them go out of hands' reach,' she'd said and told me how hers had saved her and Senator Calavia's lives during the Great Rebellion. Three minutes later, despite my cold fingers, the shackle sprang open from the padlock. I left the chain still looped through the gates with the open padlock connecting it as if closed, and ran back to the SUV.

Vibiana had dozed off. I wrapped my own thermal blanket round my legs and feet.

Now we would wait.

Nobody was chasing us that we knew; O'Keefe hadn't made good on her threat and we were five hours away from New York. I was surprised Dubnus let Vibiana go like that. I suppose she'd served her purpose. I'd found no bugs in her clothes or bag and despite her complaining I'd scanned her in her underwear as well, just to be sure. But why weren't they worried she'd go to the authorities back in Roma Nova? I didn't want to stick around here to find out.

Apart from her Roma Novan passport which was bound to be on a watch list by now, Vibiana had no papers – Dubnus had kept them – and Flavius and I were here in the EUS under false passports. I'd been forced to use my real one for the car rental and in facing off O'Keefe. I shivered. Despite my sturdy thrift shop coat, scarf, woollen gloves and hat, I felt cold. I guess I was tired. I'd driven for nearly five hours after a tense day and my eyes were prickling. It was nearly midnight. I locked the vehicle doors, lay my phone in my lap, volume set to max, inserted the headphones into my ears and closed my eyes.

The ping pierced my brain so painfully I thought my eyes would pop out. I shook my head, then looked at the screen. They were forty minutes away. Gods. I let out a deep breath which plumed in the chill. The window was covered in ice.

'Wake up!' I prodded Vibiana. 'Wake up, will you?'

'Mm?' She didn't even open her eyes. It was nearly black out there. Even the moon was shy behind the cloud cover. I checked my watch.

Five-thirty. Sunrise wasn't until just before seven. I reckoned it was safe to start the engine and warm us up. Gods, it sounded so loud, but the light frost slipped off the windows with the auxiliary heater going full blast. After five minutes, I reversed and stopped at the airfield gates.

I made Vibiana get out and open the gates, then shut them behind us once inside. I jumped out and relocked them.

'But suppose we need to get out again…' she said.

'We're not going out that way, so no problem.'

I drove up to the first hangar, but that was too open to view. So was the second. But the third was perfect, nestled behind the other two. We parked up by the side. Another ping. Twenty minutes. I wrote a note of apology to the airfield club asking them to contact the rental company to collect the SUV and charge my card. I left a hundred dollar note on the seat as a 'donation'.

A faint buzz, then a rumble followed moments later by a roar as the plane dropped out of the cloud then quickly embraced the ground. It bounced along the turf runway, taxied back, then turned ready for take-off. It had no markings but strange angles to its wings and as far as I could see in the faint light it was a dark grey with some lighter patches. A metal ladder burst out of the plane. We grabbed our bags and hurried towards it. A blue-uniformed figure beckoned us urgently. Her white cloth badge was just visible in the pre-dawn light. Imperial Air Force.

'Hurry!'

'We have one wounded and one civilian,' I called out and pushed Vibiana forward. The airwoman jumped out, grabbed Vibiana and gave her a shoulder up to the ladder. She had to do it twice and breathed heavily afterward. I bent and gave Flavius the same, but more gently, then passed the bags up. Then I heard the sirens. I peered over towards the access road. Blue and red flashing lights. They weren't New York cops – they must be feds. Gods! O'Keefe. How had she tracked us?

'Are you going to be all day, looking at the scenery? The pilot's rather anxious to go.' I jerked my head round. Then I heard that rich, sexy, masculine laugh. His face appeared in the doorway. Conrad. I grasped the lowest rung of the ladder and hauled myself up. He grabbed me and I heard the faint scrape of the retracting ladder and the slam of the door.

I opened my mouth to say something, but the senior airwoman got in first and thrust a cloth bag at me, then one at Vibiana.

'In the bag you'll find a flight suit. Put it over your first layer of street clothes and pull the hood over your head. Anything metal – earrings, watches, phones, belts – and any small stuff, put it into the bag. Your coats, give to me.'

I stripped off down to my sweater and pants, shed my metalwork and pulled on my suit.

'Not again!' Vibiana put on her bullish face.

'If you don't get that suit on within the next two minutes, you'll be out of the plane,' the airwoman retorted.

'Why should I?'

'It's a stealth plane. We need to be stealthy. That's a stealth suit. Now put it on.' She gave Vibiana such a fierce look, I was surprised she wasn't incinerated on the spot.

'What about him?' Vibiana was struggling into the flight suit and losing her balance as the plane taxied along the bumpy surface. I reached out and steadied her. She jabbed a finger in Flavius's direction. He was lying on the floor and taking shallow breaths.

'He'll be wrapped in shielding blankets. Now sit over there and don't make any noise beyond breathing.'

Surprisingly, Vibiana did as she was told. Conrad smiled in sympathy at the senior airwoman, who rolled her eyes. He took my hand and we found two jump seats away from Vibiana. It wasn't exactly luxurious, but the benefit of the stealth lining meant every surface was padded with the shielding material. The cabin went dark. I sensed Conrad bend down, then his lip touched the lobe of my ear. A tingle ran through me.

'Are you okay?' he whispered.

'Yes,' I whispered back. I was only too pleased to be on this transport, safe with Conrad.

'I'll explain when we refuel at Keflavik in a few hours. We have to go silent for the moment.'

I squeezed his hand and laid my head on his shoulder. His arm came up and folded me into him.

12
___

The landing was a lot smoother at the Keflavik air base but we taxied for an age. We had no windows, of course, but I calculated it had to be around 3–4 p.m. local time allowing for flying through several time zones. When the door opened at last, hangar lights almost blinded me. I guess it made sense to be under cover hidden from human and satellite view.

A smiling face topped with bleach blond hair appeared in the doorway. We stood and grabbed hold of the airframe struts for balance but kept back from the hatch, out of view from the outside.

'Colonel Mitelus? Captain Einar Jónsson of the Royal Icelandic Coastguard. Welcome to Keflavik Air Base. Any of your people want to stretch their legs while we refuel?' His tone was innocent, but his eyes narrowed.

'No, thank you, we're well rested and we'll be fine.' Conrad gave Captain Jónsson one of his over-cheerful smiles that batted the ball back to the Icelander. I pulled my hood further over my forehead. Although two crew needed to go outside, they wore blue disruptive pattern field caps with the peak well over their eyes. No way did we want any videos or stills of any other individual Roma Novans, military or civilians, being made for any kind of intelligence gathering. We had good relations with the Nordic League, but you never knew…

When Conrad finished the obligatory inter-service chit-chat with

Jónsson, I pointed to his neck. The fastening strip of his stealth suit had come partly undone when he'd pushed the hood off to talk to Jónsson and his fatigues jacket showed through. But instead of the black embroidered oak leaf on each collar point, there were grey lictor's fasces with protruding axe. And Jónsson had called him Colonel Mitelus.

'Yes, my promotion came through.' I saw the flash of his smile and his eyes gleam. 'Not without a fairly intense set of interviews and tests. I'll deny it,' he whispered, 'but I think Legate Vara giving me only an average report piqued the interview board's interest.'

That figured. I know he was my love, but I was very proud he had been A-rated throughout his career. To suddenly catch a mediocre report must have looked odd.

'So what are you doing here?' Senior officers who were newly promoted colonels and deputy legates didn't usually come out into the field. Not that I wasn't really pleased to see him. In the half light, his hazel eyes shone.

'Officially, I'm observing our latest stealth plane. Unofficially, I wanted to see you, of course. I also want to know what in Hades is going on with this Vibiana business and that little bastard Dubnus. But first things first.' He glanced around. The pilot and co-pilot were busy doing checks and Vibiana still had her eyes closed. He bent towards me, his throat muscles stretching under the tan skin. He pulled me to him. Through the chemical smell of the stealth suit, I smelt his warm, masculine scent. I bent back and moved my head up and my lips found his. The warmth of his mouth on mine – I wanted to devour him. His fingers shaped themselves round the back of my head as he pressed me to him. I wound my arms round his waist and clenched them together, never wanting to release him.

A cough.

'Hm?' Conrad released my lips barely enough to emit that tiny sound. I took a quick breath.

'Sorry to interrupt you, sir, but ten minutes to departure.'

Gods, how long had we been in another world?

'Oh, yes, of course.' Conrad stood up to his full height and bumped his head on an airframe crosspiece. I transformed a giggle into a cough. He frowned at me, then grinned. 'I'd better say *vale* to Jónsson. They've been very helpful.' He ran the back of his fingers down my cheek then spoke to the senior airwoman. Jónsson reappeared; they shook hands after a few words and the door shut.

We landed at Brancadorum Imperial Air Force Base rather than the military side of Portus Airport outside Roma Nova city. Flavius was taken to the airbase sick bay; he was running a fever. I hated leaving him but the air force medics would look after him for now. Conrad went forward and thanked the pilots; he left me to sort out Vibiana. I didn't know how she managed to be so disagreeable all the time. Maybe I rubbed her up the wrong way or maybe she was super grumpy by nature.

'I just want to go home. And I have to file a report with the Silver Guild and hand them over the recovered element. Why should I go with you?'

'First of all, you're still under arrest for treason under the provisions of Table Eight so you have no option.' I held my hand up before she could reply. 'And hasn't it occurred to you that Dubnus and his buddy let you go too easily? Don't take this personally, but why aren't you dead?'

'Why, you—'

'Enough.' Conrad. 'Marcia Vibiana, you are likely to be in some danger. It could be personal, legal, physical or something else. For your own protection, you are to remain hidden.' He glanced at me. 'I've messaged Countess Mitela for her permission for you to stay with us for the moment.'

None of us said anything as we rode in the anonymous sedan. Apart from the headlights and coloured glows on the instrument panel, it was pitch dark. And it was sleeting. What in Hades did Conrad think he was doing inviting Vibiana into our home? Couldn't she have gone to one of the PGSF safe houses? Well, Nonna had given her permission so I was stuck with it. Further on, the lights of the suburbs flitting by lit up their faces intermittently; Conrad's wore an impassive expression and Vibiana the usual pained one with tight eyes and turned down mouth.

The night shift security detail at Domus Mitelarum watched as the car slid in through the service entrance; they said nothing as they opened the car doors. We trudged across the back courtyard between snow piled up each side of a dark grey path carved out of the white.

I stamped my freezing feet on the sisal mat by the entrance door of the service passageway that linked kitchen, storerooms and staff quarters. Out of respect for them, I stayed silent as we walked through. The steward, Junia, met us with hot drinks. Ah, tea. The British had conquered an empire with that drink. Too bad they were moving onto coffee and soda now. Over my cup, I glanced at Conrad. He said nothing, just gave me a half smile. I wanted to shout at him, but I'd do that later.

'Welcome, Marcia Vibiana.' My grandmother stretched out her hand with one of her best smiles. 'Come and sit with me.' She pointed at the large leather couch which was my favourite perch by her side.

Vibiana hesitated. Aurelia Mitela was the senior patrician in Roma Nova and quite a presence. Only Imperatrix Silvia outranked her. Most people would be intimidated by her sense of power. But why was my beloved Nonna being so nice to this nobody?

Vibiana sat on the edge of the couch seat and clutched her mug. Maybe she was asking herself the same question.

'Colonel Mitelus tells me you need to remain covert for your own safety,' Aurelia said. 'You can be assured you will be secure here. Nobody in this household will mention your presence.' She laid her hand on the back of Vibiana's free one. 'Roma Nova owes a great debt to Maximus Vibianus for his service during the Great Rebellion. It's the least I can do to protect his great-niece.'

I stared at Nonna. Although I hadn't been born in Roma Nova, I'd studied hard and thought I knew all the main personalities of the Great Rebellion. It was thirty years ago, and Nonna had led troops liberating the country. But who was this Vibianus she was praising? Such a paragon couldn't possibly be related to Grumpy.

After such a tiring time dealing with Vibiana, I'd been looking forward to talking to Nonna. She welcomed me back, hugged and kissed me then turned all her attention to her new guest. I left them to it.

In our private quarters, I pulled off my thrift shop clothes I'd been wearing for the past twenty-four hours and threw them on the floor. I stomped into the warm shower and shoved soap all over my body. A minute later, it was plucked from my hand and Conrad's arm circled my waist. He pulled me to him and kissed the back of my neck. I leant back against him revelling in the warmth of the man and the warmth of the shower. His other hand caressed my breast, my stomach and my groin, I sighed, then gasped as his fingers explored further.

'Shh, just relax.' His voice was equally caressing. He turned me, gently pressed me against the tiles, his mouth crushing mine under the hot streaming water.

13

Just after seven the next morning, I was back in uniform and eating my eggs and bacon. Conrad smiled across the breakfast table at me. I responded automatically, remembering waking earlier enfolded in his arms. His hazel eyes reflected the warmth in his smile. I stopped, my fork halfway to my mouth, and my stomach fluttered. I forgot the rest of the world.

'If I may interrupt?' Aurelia's voice pulled us back. She inclined her head towards Vibiana, whose back was to us; all Vibiana's attention was on selecting food from dishes on the sideboard. 'What are your plans this morning?'

'I think the best thing is to go in as if I came back empty-handed and watch for reaction,' I said. 'I'll pretend to be keeping it all super secret, but leak a few words to the right people.'

'Acting as bait again,' she said.

'It's a very effective technique,' I retorted.

'Agreed, but there are obviously some very influential players behind this, Carina, so be careful who you trust.' She made a moue. 'I'm not going to apologise for saying that.'

Apart from routine stuff and a message from Daniel on his way back from the mountain exercise, there was nothing out of the ordinary waiting for me at my desk. I hung around with a cup of coffee, looking suitably subdued and catching up on news with colleagues.

'Mitela!' The adjutant. I peeled my rear off my neighbour's desk and slid into my own seat. 'Stop chatting and get your operation report on my desk by this afternoon.' He snorted. 'If you can call such a cock-up an operation.'

Heat spread up my neck into my face. I caught a few nods and rueful smiles of sympathy and one bark of laughter. Calenthus, one of Dubnus's buddies. His desk was by the side wall in the admin area.

The cavern-like general office was a pain in the butt if you wanted to have a private conversation but for once I was grateful for its open plan. Although separated from us by a half-height partition made up of low-level shelving, you could hear and see everything done by the admin and legal weenies.

I tapped away on my keyboard, churning out the required official report, but watched Calenthus out of the corner of my eye. He looked around, then over at me. I locked my eyes onto my keyboard. After a second I peeked over in his direction. He was tapping away on his phone. He could have been messaging anyone, but my suspicious mind thought it had to be Dubnus. A minute later, after he'd put his phone down, a really loud ping sang out from his direction. Not even put his phone on silent – what an idiot! He looked over at me again, looked back at his phone screen then looked again. Juno, didn't he know even the basic rules of staying covert?

A second, softer ping. He studied the screen, then looked up and openly fixed his gaze on me. He grinned. Not good.

I sent my official report to the adjutant, but wrote a second, secret one in longhand. I didn't want any trace of it in the central document registry. Dubnus's actions in North America were questionable. Only the assault on Flavius would stand up in court and that would be Dubnus and buddy's word against Flavius. Vibiana could testify against him, but apart from acting a little heavy-handed he would protest he was guarding her in the name of Roma Nova. And his absence was covered by that damned study leave travel warrant. But worst of all, Legate Vara would always take her cousin's side. No, while he might catch a disciplinary, he wouldn't be convicted by a court martial. We had to catch him *in actu*.

Getting the go-ahead from his executive assistant, I knocked on Conrad's door.

'Ah, the real facts!' he said. 'Oh gods, it's in your handwriting!'

'No need to poke at me. No way am I typing it here. Anybody might read it, including you-know-who.'

'Agreed.'

'Anything on the joint services watch list about my grumpy friend?'

'Yes.' He swivelled his screen round. Vibiana's face and profile stared out along with her description as a fugitive, and an instruction to arrest on sight for treason, economic sabotage, theft of strategic assets, handling and sale of stolen goods and evading arrest.

'I've only just filed my report. How on earth did this get out so quickly?'

'Exactly. When I sent you and Flavius to go and bring her back, the order was restricted to the confidential circulation list and she was only wanted for questioning as a person of interest. This notice on the *open* list was posted last night by the *custodes*.'

'Why? Surely being on the confidential list should have made them at least consult us.'

'You tell me. Perhaps your friend Lurio could enlighten us.' His face was neutral as he spoke the words, but his voice was coated with sarcasm. Lurio was now the local commander of the XI *Custodes* station for the central part of Roma Nova, a good promotion after his stint as the previous minister of justice's personal assistant. He and Conrad had history, not least from the time Lurio and I were briefly lovers.

'I'll ask him who requested the notice be posted,' I said.

'Go in person and tell him to forget you ever asked.'

'He will.'

'Well, you know him better than I do.'

'Why are we playing at cloak and daggers in the middle of the day?' Lurio munched on his sandwich. We were sitting on plastic padded seats in a booth at the back of a small sandwich bar used by office workers.

'Nothing of the kind – it's just a bit confidential.'

'You're in civvies, you asked me to wear a coat over my uniform and log out as if for lunch. What else would you call it?' He finished, wiped his hands on the paper serviette and leant back, waiting.

'Look, this is part of a highly confidential operation only known to a very few people. We have a, um—'

'Well, spit it out.'

'We think we have a rogue guard who's protected at high level.'

'Ha! I presume the protector isn't the upright Mitelus,' he snorted. I kicked him under the table. 'The only other possibles are his opposite number in the regulars who's too thick to do anything but work out the palace guard rota, or that blasted woman Vara.'

'I—'

'Don't bother, Bruna. It's one or the other which means it's a complete pile of shit you're digging into. I wouldn't, if I were you.'

'Too late. But I think we can shovel our way out and catch the rogue guard, but I need your help.'

'What in particular?'

'Who instructed the *custodes* to post the wanted bulletin on Marcia Vibiana on the open list?'

He blinked. His mistake.

'That's confidential.'

'How in Hades is that confidential?' I knew from my time in the *custodes* that it was a simple sign-off.

He stood, fastened his coat and stepped out of the booth, but I was there before him and blocked him.

'Sit down, Lurio, I haven't finished.'

'Well, I have.' He gave me a steady look. 'Are you going to take me on, Bruna?'

He was tall and strong. I didn't doubt my own ability, but it would make a mess. And he knew it.

'Not here. These people are innocent, I don't want to fight you, but if you don't cooperate you'll be up on a charge of treason yourself. Or obstruction at least.'

'I'm trembling already.'

'I would be, in all honesty.'

'Just leave it, Bruna. Let things take their course.' His expression was almost pleading.

'Why are you blocking me?'

'You're the one doing that,' he said. 'Now get out of my way.'

'This is ridiculous. What in Pluto is going on?' Conrad frowned. 'They can't be running an operation involving Vibiana, can they? Or are they investigating something else that's connected with silver?'

'I can't believe Lurio wouldn't tell me.' I glanced at him, then away. 'I may have a contact who can help. But it has to be totally off the record.'

His eyes narrowed. 'Who? No, on second thoughts, don't tell me. Just don't let it be traced back here.'

I climbed the stairs to the second floor of an *insula* off the Via Nova. Why she had to live in an old block with no lift was beyond me. I raised my hand to knock on the metal door when it opened.

'I spotted you coming up the stairs,' she said. 'Concealed camera.' She opened the door further and I stepped into a studio apartment that looked as if it had been raided. I nearly tripped up on a pile of discarded clothes. I scooped them up and threw them on the unmade bed. In contrast, the desk area was immaculate, no paper except for a small jotter pad, no pen except for one in a slimline desk tidy. Three highly polished full-size screens and their keyboards faced me. Their owner, however, wore a pair of jeans with slashes at the knees and frayed hems, topped with a crumpled tee showing multiple signs of coffee drinking. Her urchin cut hair and skinny figure made her look about twelve.

'Why are you here?' she said. 'I'm not on duty yet?'

'Less of the attitude, Fausta.'

'Oh, sorry, ma'am, I'm sure.'

In front of me was one of the shining stars of the PGSF IT service. To be truthful, she was a little tainted as she'd been an expert black hat hacker. Maybe more grey hat as she hadn't had the malicious intent typical of a black hat. But I hadn't shared that knowledge with the recruitment people at the PGSF as she'd put that behind her, she'd said.

'I know you're not on until this evening, but I need you to do something. Well, two somethings.'

She shot me a suspicious look. 'Illegal, I suppose?'

'I presume you can get into the city *custodes* system?'

'Illegal definitely, then.' She tilted her head. 'You'll get me a good lawyer and visit me in prison?'

'Oh, you think you might get caught? Oh, sorry, I wouldn't have bothered you. Forget I asked.' I turned towards the door.

'Wait. I didn't say I couldn't.'

I smiled to myself, then turned back with an assumed serious expression to face her. 'No trace guaranteed?'

'Not the whisper of an ant's breath,' she replied. 'What's the other thing?'

'How good are you at voiceprints?'

'I can run a cross-check against some databases if you send me the recording, but it might take a little time.' She gave me a funny look. 'Why aren't you using the databases at HQ? They've got hundreds of thousands of clean examples.'

'Look, Fausta, this is hugely covert. Only Colonel Mitelus and I are in the loop on this. I don't want a trace of this search on our systems for the same reason I need to know about that *custodes* sign-off. Trust me on this one, okay?'

She nodded, but drawn by the lines of indecipherable white characters streaming across a black background she turned back to her screen. The blue insignia of the Roma Novan *custodes* flashed up and we were in. She found yesterday's notices. How I kept myself from exploding, I didn't know.

Vibiana's wanted notice had been signed off by bloody Lurio.

14

'I am going to kill him.' I was pacing up and down Conrad's office. 'I presume my "failed mission" report was posted on the confidential part of the joint watch list, so he knew I was involved in the case. It was a relatively simple question, but he's gone straight into clam mode.'

'Perhaps it may have been better to have phoned after all rather than meeting him,' Conrad said. 'That way it may not have appeared significant.'

'Sure, maybe, but I never expected such a stupid answer.' I glanced at Conrad. 'Who gave you the instruction to go and bring Vibiana back in the first place?'

He didn't reply immediately, but tapped on his keyboard and stared at his screen.

'It came from Legate Vara's office. So now we have this notice posted before your report was written, Lurio's stonewalling and one of Vara's cousins and clients freelancing while pretending to be on study leave.'

'She'll back him.'

'Obviously. She's his patron and the Varae put the patron–client relationship before Roma Nova.'

'They make me sick.'

'Perhaps, but they've been traditionalists for sixteen centuries.' He tapped again. 'Flavius has been transferred from the sick bay at Brancadorum. Go and talk to him. If we can at least nail Dubnus for that assault in Quebec, that might worry the opposition, whoever they are.'

I made my way to the other ranks' quarters and found the *optiones* common room, door open. I knocked on the doorframe. It wasn't mandatory, just good etiquette for members of different messes to ask rather than barge in. I was surprised anybody heard me, the noise that was coming from the games area, but the senior *optio* nodded me in.

'Anybody special you're looking for, ma'am?' she asked.

I glanced at the digital display which showed who was in.

'Marcus Flavius. I see he's in.'

'Second corridor on the right, third door along on the left.' She paused. 'He limped in looking as if he'd been in the worst sort of bar brawl.'

'Just a traffic accident. You should see the other driver.' I gave her a really cheery smile, but she didn't say anything.

I knocked and went in. Flavius lay on the bed, his top half elevated by several pillows and his eyes closed. With large purple and yellow blooming everywhere, his face looked worse than it had been when I'd picked him up at the hotel in New York. Of course, I hadn't seen him in proper light since then. He stirred, but his eyes were still closed. I crept back to the door.

'Don't go,' he murmured.

I pulled a chair up, took his hand and pressed it lightly.

'I'm okay, really, just a bit tired. The medic visited earlier this afternoon and said I was recovering well.' He opened his eyes and tried to look convincing.

'Flav, you rip me a new one when I try to bullshit you, so don't try it in reverse. You look terrible.'

'Oh, thanks.'

I picked up the pills in the tray on his bedside table. Strong antibiotic. Had the cracked rib gone into his lung? The hospital in New York that patched him up would have kept him in if it had been that serious.

'Can you talk for a few moments?'

'Of course.'

'When you were beaten up in Vibiana's hotel, did you see who attacked you?'

He turned his head away and sighed.

'No. Just as I heard footsteps behind me, a bag was thrown over my head. I raised my hands to pull it off, then they really started in. Sorry.' He shifted in the bed and tried to sit up.

'Don't, Flav.'

'I feel a total idiot. I should have heard them.'

He closed his eyes and said nothing for a minute or two. He took a deep breath and winced. 'Have you contacted that kid, the cypher clerk at the Montreal legation? The one who came with me to New York?'

'Of course! He had clear sight of the two who bundled you into the trunk.' Gods, some days my brain had called a strike. I glanced at my watch. 'They'll still be at their desks.' I stood. 'I'll come back in the morning. Get some rest.'

I found the senior *optio* on my way out.

'I know this might sound weird, but would you keep an eye on Flavius, and let me know if anybody, and I mean anybody, wants to visit him? The sole exceptions are members of my response team.'

'Something I should know about, ma'am?'

'He's a witness in a case, but he's in no fit state to defend himself.'

As I walked back to the admin area, I messaged Livius and Atria in my response team, both *optiones*, to check in on Flavius if they could. I didn't think he was in any real danger, but you never knew.

I talked to Granius, the cypher clerk in Montreal, over the secure network from Conrad's office. In the selection of twenty random photos I sent him he selected Dubnus's buddy but not Dubnus. He looked stressed out enough at having to do this remote ID parade, so I didn't push him.

'I'm sorry, ma'am. I just can't remember that well.' His voice wavered. 'It all went so fast and I was concentrating on getting Optio Flavius out of the car boot.'

'Don't worry, Granius. You did very well. Could you write that up as a statement and email it to me?' I gave him one of my personal addresses in the cloud. As Granius's face disappeared from the screen, Conrad sat back in his seat and rubbed his hairline with two fingers. The stress sign.

'So basically, we still have nothing but circumstantial evidence,' he said.

'Yes, but it all adds up against Dubnus.'

'But not enough to convict. And we need to explore the bigger picture.'

'And think about what to do with Grumpy.'

Vibiana was sitting in the atrium with my grandmother, sipping a pre-dinner drink, nodding and smiling at her.

Aurelia looked up as we entered.

'Carina, Conrad, come and sit with us. Marcia has been telling me about your adventures.'

Marcia? She was calling her by her first name in less than twenty-four hours' acquaintance.

'So how is it going?' Aurelia said.

I glanced at Conrad who had fetched me a drink.

'I can't really say, Nonna. Ongoing investigation, you know.'

'How long are you going to keep me here?' Vibiana asked, back to charmless mode. I flicked through the pages on my el-pad and showed her the wanted poster. 'Gods! I haven't done any of that.' She jumped up. 'I insist on seeing my Guild. And my lawyer.'

'Sit down, Vibiana,' Conrad said. 'You make a call, send a message or step out of this house and you'll be in a custody wing and isolated before you can say Mercury. Carina and I are working like mine slaves to get to the bottom of this. We can do without complications from you.'

Vibiana looked round and saw three unsmiling faces, then to my complete surprise, burst into tears. My grandmother had Junia take her to her room and send up a supper tray.

Once they had gone, I sat opposite Aurelia and fixed her with a steady look.

'Poor Marcia,' she said. 'I fear she's overwrought.'

'I agree it's been something of a strain for her. But I want to talk about *your* part in this, Nonna.'

'Whatever do you mean?'

'Don't go all professional on me, Nonna,' I began. I looked down at my phone and selected the playback and Vibiana's disembodied voice echoed round the atrium.

'I didn't want to get either the vigiles or your lot involved but I was overruled. The head of the Silver Guild, Prisca Monticola, knows a senator on the intelligence oversight committee and they fixed it up through some covert old girls' network.'

'Interesting words. I think she must mean you, Nonna. Tell me, what exactly *was* this cosy little arrangement?'

'No need to use sarcasm, my girl.'

'I think you need to come clean, Nonna.'

Aurelia sent me a stern look, but I refused to look away. She was my beloved Nonna, but now she was a potential witness or even accessory. I had to harden my heart and maintain Praetorian mode.

She put her glass down on the little table beside her chair.

'Monticola confided in me that she needed to recover this silver processing element, but couldn't be seen to be negotiating directly. Vibiana was tasked to investigate it undercover, posing as a thief, and effect an exchange. To make it more realistic, she was posted as a fugitive, and going through the correct channels, I asked Legate Vara to send a couple of Praetorians after her, but only to look as if they were chasing her. They, you, weren't supposed to catch her.'

'Those weren't my orders, Aurelia,' Conrad said in a grave voice. 'We were told to be discreet, but to use all possible means to stop her and bring her back.'

Nonna looked towards the tall windows. A faint flush crept into her face as she frowned. 'It looks as if we've all been deceived.'

After supper, Conrad and I retired to our apartment where he put together a detention order for Dubnus and his buddy for when they returned from their 'study leave' in two days' time. I typed up my handwritten testimony and attached it along with Granius's statement. I would get Flavius's statement tomorrow morning.

'Vibiana may need that lawyer once this goes live.'

'Nonna said she's invited her Silver Guild friend, Prisca Monticola, over tomorrow, supposedly for lunch. I'm joining them to see what Monticola has to say for herself. She can see Vibiana afterwards.'

'I've very rarely seen Aurelia that embarrassed.'

'Well, we've all been played. The question is – by whom?'

15

Next morning, Vibiana was subdued, mechanically helping herself to breakfast, but leaving half of it. She made up for it in cups of coffee. Nonna told her to rest in her room or read in the library. Junia would arrange for her to have lunch in the latter.

Prisca Monticola arrived at half eleven. She was birdlike in her figure and movements. A cap of white hair over a face with prominent cheekbones and dark eyes darting everywhere. At the moment, they were on Nonna as the two of them went through kissing and hugging and the requisite greetings of old and close friends.

'You remember my granddaughter, Carina?' Nonna said. 'She's joining us.'

Monticola raised an eyebrow as her eyes ran over my uniform, but she shook hands and murmured pleasant enough greetings. We'd met at Nonna's last birthday party, but I'd been in an evening gown with elaborate hair and shiny shoes then, not beige service dress and Praetorian boots. We settled in the easy chairs in the atrium with winter sunlight shining through the tall windows.

'Now, Prisca, it's a pleasure to see you, of course,' Nonna said. 'But you must be aware I wanted to talk to you about business.'

'I'm pleased you asked me because I want to discuss this.' Monticola laid a printout of Vibiana's wanted poster on the coffee table and pushed it over towards Aurelia. 'What the hell happened? These people,' she flicked her fingers at me, 'were supposed to pretend to chase Vibiana, not blunder about and lose her. Poor girl. The gods know what's happened to her.'

'It's more complicated than that, Prisca Monticola,' I said and gave her the short version.

'Are you implying there's a leak in the Silver Guild?' Her eyebrows reached new heights and she was millimetres off snorting.

'Somebody somewhere has a motive we haven't uncovered yet, but the trail comes right back to you.'

'Am I a suspect?'

'Not yet.'

She jumped up. 'I didn't come here to be harassed.' She gave Nonna a haughty stare. 'Please ask my driver to come round. I have better things to do.' Her voice could have frozen icicles.

'Sit down, Monticola,' I rapped out. 'Or do you want to continue this interview at PGSF headquarters? Your choice.'

'How dare you talk to me like this!'

'I'm being restrained as you're my grandmother's friend, but if I don't learn now what this is about, you'll find out exactly how, er, determined I can be.'

I looked at her steadily, willing her to calm down. She was one of these brilliant types who, mostly dealing with less intelligent people, were fuelled most of the time by frustration. And they usually had hairspring tempers, just like Monticola. I was too tired to deal with prima donnas this morning.

'Prisca, do as Carina asks. This is no time for flouncing around. She wouldn't be asking if there wasn't a good reason.'

'Gods, you Mitela women are so like each other – hard as diamonds.'

'And just as sharp,' I couldn't help retorting.

'I suppose you won't be satisfied until I tell you our every last secret, will you?'

Neither Nonna nor I said a word.

Monticola plunked herself back on the couch. 'Somebody stole the central element of a prototype processor. The Guild received a message saying the thieves were willing to sell it back. Vibiana was supposed to do the deal. But that was just a cover. The priority is finding out who stole it, then fixing that particular leak.'

'Forgive me for being paranoid, but is this element really that important? Or is it some decoy you're using as bait?'

She tried to control it, but her shoulders rolled in defensively and she sucked her lips in. She glanced at Aurelia who gave her an incinerating look.

'So that's a yes,' I said. 'You didn't think to tell the truth to your old friend, Aurelia? Even though she's a senior minister and former operative. Gods in Olympus! And you think we're a load of dumb blunderers.'

'We've looked after our own affairs since the foundation,' she said in a sulky tone. 'And we didn't know how high this went up.'

Nonna looked as cross as Hades, but I couldn't stop now.

'Tell me what your suspicions are and please don't be tempted to leave anything out.'

'Is Monticola still alive?' Conrad chuckled as he listened to my recording.

'Just about. I took her into the library to see Vibiana and after all the tears and hugs, let them talk to each other quite freely. I stayed by the door and after a while I think they forgot about me. Vibiana stays with us and I told Monticola to zip her lips. I've written up my statement with a summary. It's all circumstantial, but all pointing back to Vara. The person the Silver Guild suspects is her brother's daughter.'

'Gods. But nothing direct?'

I shook my head.

He slammed his desk. 'Blast the woman.' He glanced at me. 'Don't take this out of this room, but rumour has it she's sleeping with the defence minister so I can't take our suspicions to him. Not without a bulletproof case.'

'Well, Nonna knows now, so she might be able to influence things politically. Our best bet is to sweat something out of Dubnus.'

I took a long wheelbase out onto the tarmac at Portus Airport, along with a double security detail headed by Atria from my response team. The cold breeze pushed the usual smell of aviation fuel away. Dubnus and his tagalong trotted down the first few steps, not looking too slaughtered by the overnight flight from the EUS. Then he saw I was waiting for him. He stopped halfway down, his buddy almost falling over him. Passengers behind them started grumbling and urging them on so they were forced to continue.

On the ground, he half turned as if to ignore me, but I shot my arm out to stop him. He glared at me.

'Aulus Dubnus, I am arresting you under the Military Code, Section 49A. You will be detained immediately until a military court hearing. Do you submit to the court?'

'The Hades I do!'

I beckoned one security detail forward. They pulled him away from the steps and cuffed him. His buddy dropped his bag on the tarmac and ran for it, but Atria and the other guard gave chase. She caught him with a flying tackle, landing squarely on him. The other passengers filing off the plane stared at us, rubbernecking like at a car crash. I guess it was, in a way. As the security detail prepared to push Dubnus up into the vehicle, he pulled away from them and spat on my boots. I should have been glad it wasn't in my face.

'Fuck you, Mitela. You're finished this time.'

'I doubt it, Dubnus. Not with what we've got on you. And that's "Fuck you, *Lieutenant* Mitela" to you.'

'Full detention, both of them. No visitors, none. I don't care if it's the minister of defence himself. No exceptions.'

'Okay, ma'am, I've got the message.' The custody sergeant frowned at me. I beckoned Atria over to the side wall.

'Did you get his luggage off the plane?'

'I tasked one of the detail to bring it straight here. But we can go through his cabin bag now.'

'Do it, but somewhere private, like your room, and don't do any paperwork around it. We'll let his suitcase go through the normal process, though.' I checked nobody was in earshot. 'If he's hiding anything, he'll keep it near him, so it'll be in his cabin bag. Take the whole bloody thing apart down to stitch level.'

'Looking for anything in particular?'

'No. Well, yes. Anything we can nail that bastard Dubnus with.'

I'd contacted the Interrogation Service yesterday and a senior lieutenant called Murria who I'd worked with before was standing by. I'd sent her the full file last night. She appeared within fifteen minutes and we went down to Interview 2, a grey concrete walled room with only a plastic topped table fixed to the floor and three orange bucket chairs. Two cameras watched over us, recording equipment on.

Murria leaned back and examined her nails. I stared at Dubnus for a full five minutes. He stared back for a minute, then away and finally down at his hands in his lap. Most people couldn't hold out for the minute, so I gave him a few points for that. He had been trained as a Praetorian after all. Eventually Murria sat up and flicked a sheet of paper.

'When did you start freelancing, Dubnus? We've seized your bank account details, so please don't go to the bother of lying.'

'You can't prove a thing, so no comment.'

'We have twenty-seven more days to question you and I think you'll be squawking like one of Juno's geese before then.'

She went through every bank statement and every payment in it for the past seven years. I nearly fell asleep. But there were significant unexplained deposits about which Dubnus said 'no comment'. I said nothing during this phase – Murria was the forensic expert. I went and stood behind Dubnus's chair from time to time or next to him and stared down at him with my arms crossed – classic intimidation technique, so Murria said.

Two hours after we started, Atria poked her head round the door behind Dubnus and beckoned me. Her facial expression was neutral but her eyes were gleaming. Outside in the corridor she thrust an earpiece into my left ear, the one without my comms earpiece. At the other end of the wire, the jack was sticking out of a tiny phone in her hand, a half-size version of a standard smartphone. She grinned then pressed the screen. As I listened, I grinned back. I hugged her, then went back in.

Shortly afterward a guard brought coffee for me and Murria and a cup of water for Dubnus. I took a sip of my steaming drink and breathed out in Dubnus's direction. After a few more sips, I stood up and walked over to him. I leant over him.

'Okay, Dubnus, let's continue talking about money from unknown sources,' I said. 'Who was the woman who had the element, the one Vibiana handed the money over for in New York?'

'Dunno. Never seen her before in my life. I was just there to facilitate the deal.'

'Uh huh.' I perched on the edge of the table. And fished the tiny phone from out of my pocket. He went to grab it, but couldn't with his hands shackled to the staple in the middle of the table.

'Oh,' I said. 'Did you want to make a phone call?' I smiled sweetly. 'Well, when we searched your cabin bag, guess what we found? Aren't you the careful one? Let's listen to some of the conversation you recorded after Vibiana left.'

Murria glanced at me then fixed her gaze on Dubnus, her chin forward and a pen in her hand.

'You think she swallowed it?' The New York man's voice I'd heard through Vibiana's bug at the very start of the meeting.

'Assuredly.' The Latin-speaking woman.

'And we'll be able to pressure her for more?'

'Be in no doubt, Scott Harlesen, Vibiana will be arrested the instant she steps onto Roma Novan soil on charges that will ensure her detention for a good twenty-five years. I'll get called in as the Guild's lawyer and shall make it perfectly clear to her that only my contacts will be able to stop that happening.'

'Well, my cousin Vara can keep the Praetorians off, no problem.' Dubnus's voice. He laughed. *'Providing I get my usual cut.'*

'And the custodes *will be reined in by the minister,'* the woman said. *'Now, have we concluded our business?'*

Then a crackle and no more.

The skin on Dubnus's face had lost almost all colour. His hands clenched. We waited.

'He refused to make a full confession and insisted on having a lawyer present. I told him I might think about calling one for him in the morning. He still thinks Vara will rescue him.'

'Humph.' Conrad looked over at me. 'As soon as you finish your sandwich, we'll see if Legate Vara is free for a little chat.'

'This is the end of her career, isn't it?'

'Yes, plus a lengthy sentence for economic sabotage. It's a shame we can't pin accelerated greed on her.'

'Corruption?'

'That's down to the lawyers.'

My phone pinged. A message from Fausta. *Call me urgentest!!*

'Would you mind if I made a quick call before we go upstairs? This may be a breakthrough.'

He raised an eyebrow, but nodded.

I punched in Fausta's home number and she answered instantly.

'Yes?'

She almost gabbled the findings at me.

'Good work. You sure?' I winced as she swore at me.

I glanced at Conrad. He was looking at a file on his desk trying not to appear interested.

'Keep your tunic belted,' I said down the phone. 'Okay, now listen. You need to message this information to this number and ask her to pass it on to the person who needs to know.'

Pause.

'It's my grandmother's personal phone.'

Pause.

'Are you still there?' I said.

I could hardly hear her.

'What do you mean, you daren't? Just bloody do it. She won't eat you!'

I pressed the red button, cutting her off.

'Care to share?' Conrad's voice interrupted my vision of the normally over-cocky Fausta cowering over her phone, nervous fingers composing a message to the second most powerful woman in Roma Nova.

'My, er, assistant has identified the woman handling Vibiana's deal in New York. She confirms she's a lawyer for the Silver Guild and Vara's niece on her brother's side. If she, my assistant, can get her nerve back she should be messaging this and a copy of the voiceprint to Nonna for onward transmission to Monticola.'

'Excellent! You can send my personal congratulations to your hacker, I mean assistant.' He smiled. 'This is all coming together. Monticola will prosecute the lawyer. Now we have to do the political bit – Vara – and find out about the justice minister.'

16

I tagged along with Conrad, file under my arm. He had the shitty job to do, arresting Vara. She hadn't been the legate commanding the PGSF all that long. Her career path wasn't outstanding; she'd served in the regulars, the palace guard and protection squad, but no special forces or intelligence experience. Although technically he had a selection panel to assist him, the defence minister had the job in his gift and he'd given it to his lover. Conrad seemed to take it in his stride, but my blood boiled every time I thought about it. He was a disciplined Roma Novan from birth; I was more open with my feelings. I took a deep breath as we approached the legate's office.

In the outer office Vara's executive assistant and her two clerks were tapping away at computers. She buzzed through Conrad's request for an urgent meeting and after a few seconds we were waved through.

'Good afternoon, ma'am,' Conrad began. 'Thank you for seeing me at such short notice.'

'I am in the middle of a personal crisis, but you can have five minutes.'

I bet she was, with a cousin and niece up to their ears in trouble. She frowned, which made her sharp features even more pronounced. Her brown hair, highlighted but with grey roots poking through here and there, was drawn back in a chignon. She wasn't in uniform, but I'd heard on the rumour mill that she thought herself above wearing one except when absolutely necessary. She looked a tad impatient now, but had presence, I admitted.

'It may take a little longer, but I'll keep it as brief as I can.'

She didn't invite us to sit.

'You may remember that you asked us to go to North America,' Conrad started. 'Our task was to bring back Marcia Vibiana, an academic scientist working for the Silver Guild.'

'I understand the mission failed,' she replied to Conrad, but threw me a sharp look.

'Yes and no,' he said. 'It opened up a far greater conspiracy which we have now uncovered and documented in full. The evidence is strong – unassailable, I'd say.' He stretched his hand out toward me and I handed him my file.

'Oh, really?' Vara sounded bored and started fiddling with a paperclip.

'Yes,' he said. 'I think you must know what I'm referring to.' His eyes were hard as stone. I'd only seen that look once before when I'd been undercover and he'd thought I was a drugs dealer. I shivered.

'I am going to submit our dossier to the imperial accusatrix to open a prosecution against you.'

She stood and came round to stand right in front of him.

'Don't be more stupid than you appear, Mitelus. You have no chance of succeeding.' She grasped my file, but he held on to it. 'Give me that file and I'll try to forget what you've just said.' Dark pink patches bloomed either side of her nose and her mouth hardened into a tight line.

'With respect, ma'am, no.'

She crossed her arms for a few moments, then retreated to her chair.

'I see,' she said. She shot me a hostile look. 'Send your junior out and we'll talk about it like people of the world.'

'Again, no. She was instrumental in completing the case. She is also my witness.'

'That's not valid. *Testis una, testis nulla.*' She smirked at him.

'Of course, I can easily call in another officer as a second witness. Do you have any preference?' He raised an eyebrow as if he were addressing a junior recruit. I nearly laughed, but held it in.

'What do you want?'

'I want justice done.' Conrad's tone was implacable.

'How old-fashioned!'

'No, Vara,' I couldn't help jumping in. 'It's a Roma Novan core value that you seem to have forgotten.'

'How dare you speak to me like that. I'll see you reduced to the ranks for such impertinence.'

Conrad frowned at me, but I took a step forward.

'I'm speaking to you as the Mitela heir now, so on the larger scale I outrank you by several steps. Unless you surrender, my grandmother, as head of the Twelve Families, will take it straight to Imperatrix Silvia. Would you like that?'

'Quite the little politician, aren't you, Mitela?'

'Your choice, Vara.'

'I will not be hounded out by some trumped-up charge.' She was boiling now. She slammed the flat of her hand on her desk which made everything jingle and jump.

Conrad cleared his throat.

'It's not trumped up, and you know it. I've only come here now as a matter of courtesy, but I see it was a waste of my time.' He handed me back my file, then turned towards the door. I followed him and we were nearly out when she called, 'Wait!'

We turned.

'Yes?' Conrad said.

'Suppose I could offer you a bigger prize?'

We returned to her desk.

'What bigger prize is there than the conviction of a corrupt Praetorian legate?' His voice was bitter. I wanted to comfort him in some way. He'd fought so hard to overcome the legacy of his traitorous stepfather Caius Tellus that he was almost supersensitive to any sniff of disloyalty by anybody with power.

'What about the justice minister herself?' Vara's voice came as if from a distance. Juno, was she prepared to shaft an imperial minister to save herself?

Conrad looked down at her, then pulled up a chair, gesturing me to do the same. I fished out my phone, out of her view, and tapped 'Record'.

'What are you proposing?'

'Complete and legally robust evidence of her involvement in silver dealing – mainly futures – as well as "accommodations" with traders on unregistered sales.'

Gods, so that's what the Latin-speaker, Vara's niece, had referred to in New York. What would Conrad do? This wasn't in the game plan we'd discussed earlier. Nobody spoke for a few moments.

'And you want immunity for that? As Lieutenant Mitela hinted, we have back channels to removing a minister.'

'What else do you want?' Her voice sounded as if she were eating gravel.

'You will withdraw any protection or support immediately for your cousin Dubnus and your niece, who will shortly be thrown out of her position at the Silver Guild. They will both face the rigour of the law.'

'Gods, you're like some huckster, Mitelus. Do you seriously expect me as patron to abandon my clients?'

'Your choice.'

'You will hand over your file now and you will shred and burn all evidence incriminating me and destroy all recordings. Both of you will swear on the Twelve Tables everything is deleted.'

'If we accept this arrangement we erase the parts that include your name and any reference to you. But nothing will happen until you provide the evidence against the justice minister and it is proven.'

'You're not taking that file out of this room,' she said.

'You are destined to be disappointed, Valeria Vara. I will need to be completely sure before I arrest an imperial minister. I can't take the word of a corrupt economic saboteur.'

She leapt up. I caught my breath. She hovered for a moment, then brought her hands up as if to attack him. I went to block her but Conrad signalled me to stay put.

After a moment, she went back to her chair and helped herself to a glass of water from a jug. After gulping it down, she went over to her safe. I brought my phone up and videoed her opening it. She was so upset, she didn't block my view. She extracted a blue file and as soon as she closed the safe door, I switched my camera back on audio record. She almost threw the file at Conrad.

'Here, read it through.'

He handed each sheet to me after he'd read it. Dynamite, no question.

'We will need to check this with a registered trader so that we understand some of the subtler ramifications, but I agree that this looks bad,' Conrad said. 'The worst part is using the *custodes* to do some of the dirty work, unless they were bribed too.' He looked up at her.

'I won't forget this, Mitelus.'

'I'm sure you won't. In the meantime, please restrain yourself to administrative tasks until the situation is clarified.'

17

'I'm sorry to have insisted on you taking that oath, Monticola, but these documents are *sub judice* as well as a state secret.'

She looked like an offended hen. She glanced at Nonna but found no sympathy there. I wasn't sure whether Nonna was more angry than embarrassed. I gave it about eighty/twenty. She'd never liked this new justice minister who had succeeded her old friend Aemilia Fulvia when she'd retired.

'You are as autocratic as your grandmother was when she served,' Monticola griped. 'We *can* keep a secret in the Guild, you know.'

I knew from Nonna's stories of the Great Rebellion just how secretive they could be, and with good reason, but I also knew I couldn't take a chance.

Monticola perched a pair of gold-rimmed glasses on her sharp little nose and leafed through the documents.

After five minutes, she put the file down and stared out of the window.

'Why do these people do this?' she said. Her face looked tired; aged even. 'This woman is on 160,000 *solidi* per annum as a minister, plus her 500 day-rate attendance in the Senate which probably racks up another twenty to thirty thousand, plus free travel and meals and her government pension. Most business people would kill for that. I expect she's got legal investments as well. Yet she's trying to fiddle a few thousand, a maximum of about fifty at a round count, at the risk of losing all that. Stupid woman.'

'Is it all illegal?' I asked.

'Oh, yes. Each non-registration of a transfer counts as an offence. She's made futures transactions through a non-registered and unregulated trader. The niece will be out the door tomorrow morning. Throw the book at them.'

'Is it legal, what we're doing?'

Conrad glanced at me, then over at the far wall of his office. He stood.

'Technically no, but it's a case of being pragmatic. The idea of Vara getting away with it sticks in my throat. On the other hand, we have Dubnus, the niece and the justice minister. Vara is astute to play that hand. And she knows that we know what she's done. We'll have to watch our backs for a while. Have you downloaded your recording?'

'Sorry?'

'Oh, please! I saw you video Vara opening her safe, so I assume you recorded the whole interview.'

'That would be an invasion of privacy.' I grinned at him.

He grabbed my arm, pulled me to him. His other arm circled the back of my waist and he kissed me gently, his lips teasing mine.

'You are the most shocking woman I know, but one of my best operatives. Make sure your battery's fully charged,' he said, releasing me. 'The atmosphere will be.'

'Satisfied, Mitelus?'

'Perfectly, Vara.'

It was late now, the snow falling outside the floor-to-ceiling windows in the dark of winter.

Conrad nodded at me and I held out the file. All my work, Flavius's injuries, Vibiana's behaviour and the stress on her, that poor courier in Montreal, the expense of bringing Vibiana back, my argument with Lurio and several shattered careers. I hesitated. I had to tell myself we were doing the right thing if not the totally legal thing.

'Well, Mitela, it's late, or are you having second thoughts? Have we been through all this just to have you scared of giving me a little file?' She sneered at me, but I could see her eyes were hungry for it. I gathered up my grit and plunked it down on her desk.

'Good. Now you will both give me your oath that these are the totality of the papers, that files on your systems have been destroyed, as have all recordings or videos. Show me your phones.' Conrad pulled his out and showed her the blank folder. I hurriedly killed the transmission on mine while she was concentrating on his phone. He shot a glance at me and I gave him a tiny nod. I stretched my hand out with mine, but I didn't venture any kind of smile.

We took the oath on her copy of the Twelve Tables then left. Conrad looked grim; I had such a sour taste in my gullet, I wanted to throw up.

Back in his office, he issued the arrest warrant for Vara's niece. The detail would pick her up within the hour. Monticola could send her dismissal letter to the cell block in PGSF headquarters.

'I'll see the minister in the morning, but I think we'd better warn Silvia.'

'I expect Nonna will go and see her first thing. Perhaps it would be better to coordinate with her?'

He rubbed his hairline with two fingers and nodded.

'Home. Now,' he said in a voice stripped of any feeling.

I poured a double brandy from the drinks tray in the atrium, he a whisky. But I felt so sick of the whole business, I found I only wanted a sip. I scrubbed myself clean in the shower afterwards and fell into bed with Conrad, exhausted physically and emotionally.

'What do you mean, he's gone?'

Like we hadn't anything else to do today. Conrad had gone to the palace with Nonna to warn Silvia about the arrest of her delinquent minister and had a frosty reception apparently. But the arrest order was to be executed within the hour. Now the custody sergeant was telling me Dubnus had been sprung.

'Exact details, please.'

'I know you said nobody, ma'am, but it was the legate.'

'What!' The anger rolled up through me and I couldn't speak for a few moments. So much for Vara's agreement.

'When was this?'

He flipped through his log onscreen. 'Yesterday lunchtime. He came back from interrogation, Lieutenant Murria signed him back to us. Half an hour later, Legate Vara signed him out on her personal recognisance.'

Just before Conrad and I went to see her. Pluto in Tartarus! That bloody woman. She'd sat there all that time we were dealing and she'd already had him safely away. I messaged Conrad. Seconds later, his reply was unprintable. He ordered an immediate search of Vara's home, Dubnus's room here in the other ranks barracks, his buddy Calenthus's room. My earpiece pinged.

'I'm on my way to see Vara.' I could hear the anger rocketing through his voice. 'Get Dubnus's apprehension entered on the Joint Watch List stat and message Lurio to take personal charge for the *custodes*, then get out there and join the search.'

Lurio grunted when I called him.

'I suppose you want an apology,' he said.

'Yes, later. You can go down on your knees and grovel, but at the moment I want everything locked down – trains, airport, all border posts. Immediately.'

'I've just seen the Joint Watch List. Wait one.'

I heard tapping on a keyboard.

'Done.'

'Will you be sending us a new minister soon?' Lurio said.

'Fuck off, Lurio.'

'You too, Bruna.'

Reports rolled in within the hour. No sign of Dubnus at the three locations; search groups were taking his and Celanthus's rooms apart, Celanthus was in an interrogation room with Murria and forensic staff searching his and Dubnus's computers and Celanthus's phone. Vara's house steward had been troublesome, but they had 'quarantined' him, then made the search.

I was buckling on my light webbing set and vest when Conrad strode into the watch room. I didn't want to ask him in front of the command staff, so I just raised one eyebrow. He shook his head and clenched his fist. He pulled me to one side.

'One day, I'll be kneeling in the sand waiting for the blade for that woman,' he whispered. His face was hard, his eyes like stone. 'I'll tell you the details later, but basically, she shrugged it off.' He nodded towards the screens. 'Anything?'

'Zilch.'

'Where are you going?'

'I'm meeting Daniel and a detail at Dubnus's mother's place out on the Aquae Caesaris road. It's on the obvious list, so we can't not search it.'

'Very well.' He looked at his watch. 'You should get there and back including a search within a couple of hours, three at most. We'll have a catch-up then. Murria will have sweated something out of Celanthus by then and the search teams should have finished. Even the *custodes* might have something to report if they've shifted their arses sufficiently.'

18

It was freezing, but at least the snow had stopped and the road had cleared into two sets of grey lines in the white landscape. We were only two weeks from Saturnalia and then the solstice. As my breath plumed in the sub-zero temperature, I prayed we wouldn't have an even worse January.

I spotted Daniel's long wheelbase parked under trees some twenty-five metres away from the entrance to Dubnus's mother's place.

'Morning,' Daniel said, pulled off his helmet and kissed me on both cheeks. Somebody gave a low whistle, abruptly cut off. It didn't mean anything. Daniel was one of my closest comrades-in-arms.

'Any sign of activity?' I asked.

'None, but I sent a scout forward and she saw a light on in one of the tower rooms.'

'Okay. What do we know about the mother?'

'Malendra Dubna, works in Aquae Caesaris, manager in a scientific consultancy, unlikely present. No partner. Subject's father, Gnaeus Varus, lives in the city, unlikely present.' Daniel closed his notepad.

'You happy to take the back?'

He nodded and tabbed off down the road with four of his team. I'd brought Atria and Livius, my two best *optiones* after Flavius. We'd give Daniel five minutes to get into position.

'Have you seen Flavius this morning?' I said to Atria and Livius while we waited, trying to avoid the icy drips from the trees.

'He had a good night and was going to the physio today,' Atria answered. He's furious about missing all the fun.' She grinned. Livius dug her in the ribs and smiled back at her. A ping in my ear. Daniel was in position.

'Right, let's go put an end to Dubnus's own fun. If he's here.'

A short driveway led to a single-level extended farmhouse which had at least one wing going back at ninety degrees. On the front, at the other end, a large round tower, older than the rest of the building judging by its cruder stonework. No light from any of its small windows and none from the main building. We huddled in the shrubs waiting for any reaction.

'Aquila Zero to Aquila One. Anything?' I whispered.

'Negative,' replied Daniel.

'Proceeding into main building. Meet you there. Out.'

I took a good breath, flicked my fingers at the other two and we ran for the wall by the main door. Atria hovered by the hinge, Livius by the door edge, me behind him. I nodded and he stepped back, raised his booted foot and rammed it against the lock. The door quivered but didn't give. He unslung a nylon bag, fished out a short metal tube the size of a forearm, flipped the handles up and rammed the lock. We were in.

We panned around the open-plan area, our weapons ready. With my fingers, I signalled Livius left and Atria right. I went straight through to the kitchen area and the half-glazed back door. I couldn't see anybody outside.

'Aquila Zero, suggest you come here.' Livius's voice in my ear. I trotted through the sitting area to a small hallway with a convex exposed stone wall – the tower. In the middle was a solid metal door.

'*Merda,*' I said. 'Can you open it?'

'It looks solid, but I can try round the latch area,' Livius said. 'Sometimes the frame can be weak as well. Stand back, ma'am.'

He swung the door ram with maximum force, but it just made a dent. Livius dropped the ram, ripped his gloves off and rubbed his hands.

'*Merda*, that's hard.' He examined the lock area. 'That's been reinforced to bank standards. I bet that's a solid door, not just the usual hollow one. We need a specialist.'

'Call one stat.'

Out of the corner of my eye, I saw Atria letting Daniel in through the now unlocked back door.

'Problem?'

'Yeah, short of blowing it up completely, we can't access this tower.'

'Well, there might be another way in. Fancy a climb?'

It was lower than the inner courtyard wall of the old fortress building we'd raced up only three weeks before, and rougher built so had many more foot- and handholds. Just under the eaves of a slate roof was a window with a wooden balcony. Our target. I doubted that Conrad would object to us scaling this wall. We were climbing in light battle dress but I abandoned my weapons other than my faithful Glock and my knives. It was easy-going until the first bullet flew past my eye.

'Covering fire,' I shrieked as I scuttled sideways. I looked down. The troops on the ground ran for shelter into the shrubs then sent off rounds in the direction of the window. A few more metres and we were under the wooden balcony under the window which followed the curve of the tower. I tugged on the wood with my gloved hand and part of the balcony floor came away easily enough. Rotted through. Damn. I watched as the piece dived to the ground.

I climbed higher so I was level with the balcony rail and put my foot on it, tentatively at first, gradually shifting more of my weight onto it. It held. I closed my eyes for an instant in relief. Both Daniel and I were sheltered by the curve of the tower, but the moment we got to that window, whoever was in the tower would see us and shoot us.

The covering fire was less frequent, but more precise. That had to be Livius. He was aiming at the crosspieces on the window to weaken them. If that glass was toughened or armoured, we'd be stuffed.

A volley from below. I pointed to myself with one finger, to Daniel standing on the opposite rail with two. I whispered into my comms set.

'Let's do it.'

I grasped my Glock in my right hand, pulled my half visor down to protect my face and threw myself through that window left shoulder first. The glass exploded. The crash of it nearly deafened me. Daniel thumped in after me. Glock ready, crouching, I was catching my breath, but nobody was there. An old-fashioned rifle lay on the floor. The door was ajar.

Advancing cautiously, Daniel went through. I was right behind him but I didn't see the iron bar swish through the air and thump Daniel on his helmet until too late. He dropped like a bag of grain and fell, bumping down a spiral staircase.

I shrank back into the little room. Two options: wait for reinforcements or try to reason with whoever was wielding that iron bar. Neither appealed so I took the third option and launched myself straight through the door at the iron bar wielder.

Dubnus. Of course.

He fell back onto the stairs, arms and legs akimbo. The iron bar clattered down the stairs past Daniel's slumped body, glancing off it and disappearing. I swung my head back just in time to see Dubnus spring up and come at me. I stepped back, tripped, forgetting there was a step up, and recovered by rolling back into the room. My elbow cracked on the hard floor and the Glock fell from my nerveless fingers.

Merda.

Dubnus swooped on it. He thrust the barrel into my face. I froze.

'Not so clever after all,' he said. His voice was triumphant.

I said nothing. No way was I going to rise to that.

'Can't hack it when it comes to it, then?'

'We're not finished yet,' I replied.

'Even you aren't dim enough to think your friends will get through that door for days. I should have finished you and Flavius in Montreal when we knocked that girl over in the metro station. But you didn't show up and we didn't have time to hang around.'

'What do you want, Dubnus?'

'A safe passage out of here, then out of Roma Nova.'

I actually laughed. 'You have to be joking. '

'I don't think so. I've got enough stashed away abroad to live very nicely.'

'They'd come after you. But you know the rules – no hostages, so you can kiss your ass for that way out.'

'You think they're going to let me harm their little princess? Mitelus? Your grandmother the senator? The imperatrix?'

I strained not to blink. No, they must not deal with this heap of shit. But I had to stall him for a few more life minutes.

'Tell me something, Dubnus, why do you hate me so much?'

'You haven't worked it out, have you?'

'No, I'm too dim, as you said.'

'You took my job.'

'What?'

'You sailed into it after your escapade on that mountainside shooting at a few poor sods doing their time in Truscium.'

'They were breaking out of prison and their leader was a vicious murderer.'

My half-brother, Jeffrey Renschman, who had wanted to destroy me to take our father's money.

Dubnus whacked my forehead with the pistol butt. Dazed for a moment, I shook my head.

'I was in for that officer vacancy when, thanks to you, Robbia was chucked out,' he continued. 'But you parachuted into it from being a scarab. You hadn't slogged your way up for five years. My cousin Vara said that job was mine, then there you were, Little Miss Privilege. I nearly got you on that rope bridge.'

His eyes glittered.

'Well, I'm not going to miss this time.'

I flinched and put my left hand up as if to ward him off. He took aim. He could hardly miss at this range. Gods. In a nanosecond, I snatched my carbon knife from my back waist holster and hurled it at him. He shrieked as the knife embedded itself in the back of his right hand. I flung myself flat on the floor as the Glock fired.

He writhed on the floor, the fingers of his left hand clawing at the knife and eyes streaming. Jumping up, I recovered my pistol from where it had fallen out of Dubnus's hand. He was attempting to struggle up, so I drove my fist down onto his nose. Bones crunched. He screamed and clutched his face with his good hand. I pulled my knife out of his right hand. He thrust it into his opposite armpit and rocked from side to side.

'Turn over,' I shouted at him. He stared up at me with hatred in his eyes. I stuck my pistol in his face. He released his hand and tensed. 'Don't even think about it, Dubnus. You nearly tipped me off that rope bridge to my death in the valley below, you've beaten and injured my colleagues, you've framed an innocent woman and conspired against Roma Nova. One hint of a wrong move and I'll shoot you like the pig you are. Or I could watch you bleed to death from that knife wound.'

Although his hand and face were covered in blood, and probably hurting like Hades, he wasn't in any real danger. A few moments ticked by. He slumped. I holstered my weapon and turned him over with my foot. I knelt and cuffed him, then grabbed a field dressing from my sleeve and bound it tight over a pressure pad round his hand. The bleeding had slowed, but I didn't want the medics giving me a hard time.

A groan behind me. I craned my neck round the curve of the spiral staircase. Daniel was sitting up, struggling with his helmet strap.

'What the hell was that?'

'Oh, a little tap with a toy stick,' I said and grinned at him. He stuck his tongue out at me, then grinned back. I studied his face. He looked okay, but paler than usual. I'd make sure he went for an X-ray all the same. Dubnus had really thumped him hard.

A ping in my ear.

'Aquila Two. Everything good in there, Aquila Zero?' Livius.

'Affirmative. One casualty, slight bleeding, one military mild concussion. Both for evac. Looking for the key. Back soon. Out.'

It was ridiculously easy. I rifled through Dubnus's pockets, avoiding his feeble attempts to kick me. Nothing. But as I stood up, I spotted a row of hooks above the desk and there was the key dangling directly in my sight line. Telling Daniel to watch Dubnus, I trotted down the spiral stairs to the beaten earth ground floor.

'Stand back from the door, Aquila Two,' I ordered Livius via my mouth mic. I inserted the key, turned it three times, seized the handle, depressed it and opened it to a group of astonished faces. A civilian kneeling with a drill in his hands gaped at me. 'Oh, have I spoilt your fun?' I said.

Livius chuckled and gave me a hearty tap on my outer upper arm. He took a step back and let the medical team through.

19

'It was about a job?' Conrad sounded incredulous.

'I had the impression it was boiling for some time. He missed out twice on promotions, but scraped through on his senior's recommendation each time. Guess who? And he had the nerve to say I was advancing through privilege!' I glanced at Conrad. 'I'm not, am I?'

It gnawed away at me when I was tired and sensitive to pointed remarks about the unit commander being my contracted partner.

'No, not at all. If anything, I'm a little harder on you. That's why you and Daniel ended up in the cells for a week for disobeying standing orders about that damned wall.'

Which was now fenced off.

The justice minister's trial was short but sensational. Vara's file was solid and the imperial *accusatrix* was suitably unctuous as she asked the court for the maximum penalty.

Nonna didn't comment much about it. I guess having such a key member of the government go down for corruption hit them all. Dubnus's hearing was mercifully a court martial, press excluded. Vibiana was composed as she answered questions about her deposition, but as she left the room, she looked at me and frowned. No change there. All the charges against her were deleted. Lurio didn't make any comment when he confirmed it had been done. I was still sore at him for not telling me about the justice minister gagging him.

Conrad wouldn't tell me much about his brief interview with Vara afterwards, but he didn't think she'd be much longer in post. Apparently, she'd made him swear again that all documents had been destroyed and all recordings deleted. I didn't have the heart to tell him that Fausta still had copies.

I went home the evening after Dubnus's court martial, tired into my bones. At the supper table, we talked about nothing in particular, but just as the meat was served, a wave of nausea ran up my throat and I just made it to the bathroom.

'You not only climbed that bloody wall, you let me send you on a mission while you were pregnant?'

I thought he was going to explode, but he sat stone still. Nonna said nothing, but Helena took a gulp of wine and stared at me.

'I didn't have the faintest idea until I did a test the morning Monticola came to lunch.' I looked into the distance, then back at my food. 'It's not as if I was a long way along. And I was perfectly healthy with Allegra.'

'You're grounded then, training and admin only.'

'Hello, I'm pregnant, not ill.' I glared at him. 'And would you treat any other woman soldier differently?' I had him there.

'If I may?' Nonna's cool voice cut through the rising heat. 'Carina is perfectly correct. She should be effective for at least another eight weeks. I went out into the field when I was pregnant both times and only stopped when I became operationally impacted.'

Conrad went to say something, but glanced at me instead, a puzzled expression on his face. Like me, he couldn't have believed what he'd heard. Helena turned her stare from me to Nonna who was eating her food as if she hadn't dropped a bombshell.

'*Both* times, Nonna?'

'Your mother was my only living child, but there was another who was lost in the shades before she entered the world.'

Nonna had told me about my mother's father, her childhood, her growing up and meeting my father, although I was sure she had left a load of the grimmer details out. But who was this other baby's father? I looked at Conrad who made a tiny shake of his head. Helena's eyes widened and she gave a tiny shrug. I looked at Nonna, but she gave me a grave, closed look. No way was she going to tell us more. I didn't have the nerve to push it.

She beckoned a servant and instructed her to bring some of her best Brancadorum champagne.

As the bubbles ran to the top of our glasses, mine regrettably only half filled, Nonna proposed a toast.

'*Macte* to you, Carina and Conrad, for a successful mission and congratulations on the forthcoming addition to the Mitelae of Roma Nova.'

WOULD YOU LEAVE A REVIEW?

I hope you enjoyed CARINA, the danger, adventures and passions.

If you did, I'd really appreciate it if you would write a few words of review on the site where you purchased this book.

Reviews will really help CARINA to feature more prominently on retailer sites and let more people into the world of Roma Nova.

Very many thanks!

INCEPTIO FIRST CHAPTERS

Enjoy CARINA? Read how Karen Brown first came to be in Roma Nova and how she became Carina – the start of the adventure…

I

The boy lay in the dirt in the centre of New York's Kew Park, blood flowing out of both his nostrils, his fine blond hair thrown out in little strands around his head. I stared at my own hand, still bunched, pain rushing to gather at the reddening knuckles. I hadn't knocked anybody down since junior high, when Albie Jolak had tried to put his hand up my sobbing cousin's skirt. I started to tremble. But not with fear – I was so angry.

One of the boy's friends inched forward with a square of white cloth. He dabbed it over the fallen boy's face, missing most of the blood. Only preppy boys carried white handkerchiefs. Aged around eighteen, nineteen, all three wore blazers and grey pants, but their eyes were bright, boiling with light, cheeks flushed. And their movements were a little too fluid. They were high. I dropped my left hand to grab my radio and called it in. Passive now, the second boy knelt by the one I'd knocked down. The third one sat on the grass and grinned like an idiot while we waited. If they attacked me again, I had my spray.

Keeping my eyes fixed on them, I circled around to the slumped figure lying a few steps away on the grass. Their victim. I laid two fingers on his neck and thankfully found a pulse. After a glance back at his tormentors I bent my face sideways and felt his breath on my cheek. He groaned and his body tensed as he tried to move. A battered brown felt hat lay upside down by the side of his head of long silver and black hair stiff like wire. He opened his eyes. Dull with sweat and grime, the red-brown skin stretched over high cheekbones showed he had to be an Indigenous. Well, damn. What was he doing this far east, away from the protected territories?

Path gravel crunched as Steff appeared through the cherry blossom cloud, driving his keeper's buggy with Tubs as shotgun.

'Karen?'

'One with a bloody nose, and all three for banning. Tell Chip I'll do the report as soon as I finish here.'

They herded the three delinquents onto the buggy. Before they left, I helped myself to dressings and swabs from the emergency kit in the buggy trunk. I had to see to their victim. He sat up and put his hand to his head. He shrank back, his eyes full of fear. when he saw me. Maybe it was my green uniform, with its park logo and 'Autonomous City of New York' stamped on the shoulder.

My hand started to throb, but I managed to unscrew the top of my water bottle and gave it to him.

'C'mon, old guy, drink this.'

He lifted his face, grabbed the bottle and drank it in one go. His Adam's apple bounced above a grimy line on his neck around the level of his disintegrating shirt collar. And he stank. But, right now, he needed my swabs and Band-Aids. Under a diagonal cut on his forehead, a bruise was blooming around his eye to match the one on his jaw. His hand was grazed, with bubbles of blood starting to clot. I cleaned his wounds, speaking calming words to him as I bandaged him up.

'Okay, let's get you to the nearest hospital,' I said, but, as I lifted my radio again, he seized my wrist.

'No,' he said.

'It's okay, there's a free one, the other side of the park in Kew Road West.' Which was just as well, as he plainly couldn't pay private.

'No. Thank you. I'm well. I can go now.'

The anxious look in his dark eyes swung between my face and the safety of the tall trees. I'd have to call in for the Indigenous New York Bureau number. As I spoke to Chip, I looked over the lake at the old wood boathouse on the far side. Beyond the trees behind it, the windows in the red-brick Dutch highhouses along Verhulst Street threw the full sun back. When I turned around at the end of my call, the old man had disappeared.

'You did okay, Karen,' Chip said later in his office. 'Little shits. They've been processed and taken to the south gate. I checked with the Indigenous Bureau for reported wanderers, but they had none listed.' He grinned at me. 'Jeez, the woman there was so prickly and made me feel like Butcher Sherman.'

Every kid knew from school the Indigenous had been more or less protected until the British finally left in 1867, but that, almost as the door shut, a rogue officer in the new American army ordered the massacre of Sioux and Cheyenne on an industrial scale. A hundred and fifty years on, the Indigenous Nations Council in the Western

Territories still reacted like it was yesterday. I was more than pleased I hadn't had to make that call.

I filed my report among the pile of paper in Chip's in-basket and thought nothing more of it until, after a tedious week shut in my office at my regular job, I was back on duty in the park the next weekend.

That Saturday morning, I changed into my green pants and tee in the locker room and pinned on my team leader badge. The May sunshine would bring out people in droves. I picked up my volunteer's folder from the wall rack. Hopefully, I was back on meet-and-greet supervising, instead of patrol. I could walk all day in the fresh air, greeting visitors, giving directions, answering park-related questions, laughing with the sassy kids, and helping the lost and crying ones find their parents. I knew every corner of the park from north to south, the history back to Vaux and Olmstead, who'd founded it with a huge grant from the Royal Kew in England.

I hummed a little tune and anticipated the sun on my skin. But all there was inside the folder was a note to report to the park director. What was that about? I'd met him twice before when I'd been awarded commendations, but never seen him around the park itself. Not weekends.

The sour expression on his face told me I wasn't here for an award. Chip stood with his back tight into the far corner, no sign of his usual jokey grin. I was not invited to sit on the green-padded chair this side of the director's desk.

'Miss Brown.' The director frowned at the sheet of paper in his hand. He looked up. 'Show me your right hand.' He spoke in a hard, closed tone.

He took hold of my hand and twisted it over, not caring that I winced. He glanced at the purple and yellow skin around my knuckles, grunted and let go.

'You are dismissed from the Conservancy Corps, with immediate effect. Hand your uniform, ID and any other park property to your supervisor and leave within the next thirty minutes. You have become an embarrassment to the Autonomous City of New York. We cannot stop you as a member of the public entering the park, but you will be watched. That is all.'

I stared back at him and grasped the back of the chair.

'But why are you kicking me out? What have I done?'

'Assaulting a respectable member of the public as he and his friends were quietly enjoying a walk is completely unacceptable. Even more so when drunk.'

'Drunk? How dare you!' I was hot as hell with fury. 'They were all high as kites and attacking a defenceless old Indigenous.' I took some deep breaths. 'I did what the training said. I remonstrated with them. I attempted to mediate. I placed myself between them and their victim. It's all in my report.' I threw an urgent look over at Chip, desperate for his support. He looked away.

'Have you quite finished?' The director looked at his watch.

'No, I haven't! The lead one took a swing at me. I ducked. He went for me again, so I hit him on the nose. You know I'm within my rights to defend myself.' But this was the first time I'd ever had to do it all the years I'd volunteered here. Unlike others, both volunteer and regular, I'd chosen not to carry a nightstick when I was assigned patrol.

'This interview is finished.' He nodded to Chip who stepped forward, took me by the arm and ushered me out with a murmured, 'C'mon, Karen.'

'What the hell happened there? How can he do that? And I wasn't drunk. Ask Steff and Tubs. It was eleven in the morning, for Chrissakes!' I threw my folder on his desk. 'If it wasn't so stupid, I'd kill myself laughing.'

Chip shifted his weight from one foot to the other, no grin, his easy fidgeting gone. 'You bloodied the nose of External Affairs Secretary Hartenwyck's son. He's fuming. And Mrs Hartenwyck's not only on the board of trustees, she's a major patron of the park.'

I sucked my breath in. Hartenwyck, the second most powerful person in the country. My heart pounded with fear. I closed my eyes and shook my head. He was from one of the old Dutch families, a privileged class who still called the shots even two hundred years after their last governor had sailed out of the harbour in 1813. Even though the British had stepped up from number two position and taken everything over for the next fifty years, the 'Dutch mafia' still ran everything today. And I had a British name. I didn't have a chance.

'Then they should make sure Junior doesn't take drugs,' I said. 'Or beat up old Indigenous in a public place. The Indigenous Nations Council would wipe the floor with him.'

'But you can't produce the old man to testify.'

'Steff and Tubs saw him.'

'They've been told to shut their mouths if they want to keep their jobs.' He looked at me, almost pleading. 'They've both got families, Karen.'

I walked back and forth in front of his desk, waving my arms around, but I sensed it was no use. The decision had been made and Chip was stuck with executing it.

'So, my four years' volunteer service and two commendations aren't worth jack-shit?'

He fixed his gaze on the scuffed door panel directly over my shoulder. 'I'm so sorry.'

Heat prickled in my eyes, but I was not going to cry. I wouldn't give him the satisfaction. I walked out, shut the heavy oak door with supreme control, changed back into my jeans and tee in the locker room and left the staff building, my head up. I threw the green park uniform and ID in a public trashcan. Childish, but satisfying.

II

Back at my apartment, I made a cup of tea and sat at the tiny table by the window for three hours. A whole slice of my life had been cut out in a few minutes by some rich-kid druggie. I'd loved the openness of the park, the stunning trees, kids playing naturally, the illusion of being in the country. Not the Nebraska of my teens, but New Hampshire with Dad before he died. Those weekends when we hiked and camped, surrounded by the fresh, warm air, the two of us alone. Then the day came when he lay in the hospital bed, skinny thin with his face shrunken like an old man, struggling to whisper my name. As I left the hospital that evening, when he'd fallen into his last sleep, it had rained and the air was sullen. I felt my throat tighten. The pain of losing him was as raw today as it had been all those years ago. I bit my fingernails, gulped, dropped my head in my hands and burst into sobs.

It had to be a mistake. I swallowed my pride, gathered up my grit, like Dad used to say, and spent most of Sunday drafting a respectful mail to the director asking to be reconsidered.

I blinked when a reply hit my inbox within forty minutes.

From the desk of the Director

Madam,

In reference to your recent communication, the Director finds the contents unacceptable and untrue. All allegations or claims against the Constituency of New York and all permissions and privileges are hereby rejected. Your record of attendance has been deleted.

The consequences of harassing municipal and public employees are severe and constitute a Class E Non-Violent Felony (CNY Penal Code S180).

You are advised that, on advice from the Department of Internal Security, your name has been placed on a national security watch list because of your antisocial behaviour and foreign parentage.

I stared at the screen. I felt like I'd been struck in the face. This couldn't be happening. I wasn't a terrorist or criminal. Sure, my mother had been born abroad in Europe, but she'd been dead for twenty-one years. My father was born in England but had been a naturalised American for nearly two-thirds of his life, even decorated for war service in North Africa. That kid being pissed at me couldn't have gone this far, could it?

I started shaking.

God. What else could these people do to me?

The next morning, at my regular job, I drooped over my desk and shuffled papers in folders, but I didn't know what I was doing. I worked Monday to Friday at Bornes & Black, a Connaught Avenue advertising agency handling niche inventor accounts. Pretty mundane in the two years I'd been here, but it nearly paid the bills and gave me – no – *had* given me precious free weekends in the park.

Damn.

'Hey, Karen.' A paper ball landed on the back of my right hand. I looked up. Across from me, Amanda, the other assistant account executive in our team, grinned and tipped her chin up at me.

'What's up? Eat a lemon, or did you get a tax bill?'

'No, nothing.'

She rolled her large brown eyes, but before she could open her mouth to start an interrogation, the boss's assistant materialised in front of me. This god-like being had never before looked at me, let alone smiled at me. Maybe calling it a smile was stretching it. I was to report to the boss 'at my earliest convenience' to talk about a special project. The immaculate figure turned about in a swirl of dark blue, the tail of a green and yellow silk scarf dripping down her curved, swaying back.

Amanda and I both stared.

I pushed my hair behind my ears, brushed the front of my skirt to ease the creases out, grabbed my notebook and scuttled after her. What could the boss want from me? I was nobody. With no college degree, I had watched with second-hand pleasure, but a twinge of envy, as others overtook me. But it hadn't seemed so important; I had lived for the park. Maybe I needed to change that now.

I stumbled out of the boss's office an hour later, head whirling. After nearly two years, they'd pulled me out of the herd and given me my chance. I was to make the pitch presentation to new, and important, foreign clients. Back at my desk, I stared at my notes, terrified at the responsibility, but thrilled to be chosen.

I slogged away researching, drafting and reworking my material over the following four days. I practised in front of the mirror to get it word-perfect. I worked on it over the weekend; I had nothing else to do.

Now the day of the meeting had arrived. I glanced again at my watch, checked my face again, happy that my hair was still in the elegant chignon I had persuaded it into this morning. I knew my new blue linen suit was right – the vendor in Nicholson's had said so.

Unable to bear waiting any longer, I got up from my desk. Amanda squeezed my hand and said, 'Go, girl.'

I had made the long walk into the conference room but my hands wouldn't stop trying to rearrange the neat stack of paper in front of me. I gulped some water to relieve my parched throat. Hayden, the boss, glanced over at me, one eyebrow raised. He was English. Proper English, not one of the 1860s left-behinds. His old-fashioned sports jacket and pants made him look like a crusty old guy from a black and white movie, but he gave me a human-enough smile.

The new clients came from Roma Nova, where my mother had been born. I couldn't remember too much from the Saturday class my dad had insisted on, so I was curious about what they'd be like. Checking off 'Latin (elementary)' in the language ability section on my application had seemed so irrelevant two years ago. Now it was my springboard.

A buzz on the intercom, and the door of the glass-walled conference room opened. Hayden and I rose to meet them. A short, brown-haired man walked past Hayden and held his thin hand out to me. Hayden nodded at me, nursing a half-smile, and made the introductions. This was our inventor.

'*Salve*, Sextilius Gavro,' which was about as much Latin as I could muster at that precise moment.

'My interpreter, Conradus Tellus,' he said in a sing-song tone.

His colleague was more than striking – blond hair long enough to slick back behind his ears. And tall. Several inches taller than me, even. Above a smiling mouth and a straight nose marred by a scar, his eyes were tilted slightly upwards, red-brown near the pupil, green at the edges. He fixed his gaze on me like he was measuring me up, assessing me. I refused to break, but felt warmth creeping up my neck into my face as he widened his smile. A little flustered, I eventually looked down at his outstretched hand but hesitated. I gave myself a mental shake, threw myself into businesswoman mode and stretched out my own hand to meet his.

Over the next two hours, the interpreter's gaze tracked me as I moved to the screen on the back wall and around the table, giving out mock-ups and sales projections. He asked me to pause now and again so he could interpret, but when he had finished each time, he flashed me a half-smile. Sextilius Gavro scribbled notes ceaselessly, his fingers twitching with nervous energy. He kept looking up from his papers and fixing me with a stare. Although I described market segmentation, platforms and the importance of usability in full detail, they still asked so many questions. I was a prisoner under interrogation.

I only realised hours had passed when my stomach bubbled; it was running on empty. I stopped talking. I had nothing else to say.

After they'd left, I sank back into my seat and shut my eyes for a few moments. My pulse was still pushing adrenalin around my body.

'Your research was excellent, Karen,' Hayden said, his face serious. 'More importantly, the Roma Novans were impressed by your ideas.'

I flushed. 'I was just concentrating on getting my pitch right.'

I sipped my dose of coffee. I glanced over at the papers strewn over the large, gleaming table like so much ticker tape left after a parade. That was all it came down to after days of solid work.

I rode along more familiar ground that afternoon, briefing the art director and marketing team. I needed to have the draft campaign plan ready for approval for the next client encounter in two weeks, so I settled down and attacked my keyboard.

A while later, my stomach growled. It would be home-time soon. Amanda had gone a while ago. I glanced at the clock. How could it be past seven? I was alone in the open-plan office – except for the IT engineer in the corner, and he was a geek. I had gotten lost in my so-called boring job. I smiled and admitted it felt good.

I treated myself to gnocchi *marinara* and a glass of red at Frankie's on my way home. I didn't run into anybody I knew. I didn't really expect to: New York was a city of isolated strangers, smiling outwardly but all intent on their individual universes. I was savouring the fruit-laden tang of the wine when the interpreter invaded my head. Sure, his English was excellent, British-sounding, but just a little too perfect. He wasn't an interpreter; that was way too ordinary. Self-assured, nonchalant even, he had watched everything and missed nothing.

Next morning, I was immersed in developing the implementation outline when the harsh ring from my desk phone broke through. I grabbed the handset and struggled with untwisting the cord.

'I hope you don't mind me calling you at work, but I wondered if you'd like to meet for a drink or some dinner on Saturday.'

The interpreter.

'I'm sorry, but I don't date clients on principle.'

'I didn't mean a date; simply as colleagues.'

I heard an undertone of laughter in his voice.

'No, I don't think so,' I said.

'Out of your comfort zone?'

I gasped. What was that supposed to mean?

'Sorry,' he said before I could slam the handset down. 'That was rude of me. But will you still come?'

I hadn't been asked out to dinner in six months. Why the hell not?

———

INCEPTIO is available as an ebook on Amazon, iBooks, Kobo and Nook and as a print book from online retailers or through your local bookshop.

HISTORICAL NOTE

What if Julius Caesar had taken notice of the warning that assassins wanted to murder him on the ides of March, and lived to become the first Roman emperor? Suppose Elizabeth I had married and had children? Or Napoleon had won at Waterloo? And suppose part of the Roman Empire had survived into the modern age as a new Rome – Roma Nova? Questions that have and will continue to keep us occupied for decades, if not centuries.

Few readers like a history lesson in the middle of a thriller so for my setting of Roma Nova I have dropped pieces of its background 'history' into CARINA only where it impacts on the story. But if you *are* interested, read on...

What happened in our timeline

Of course, our timeline may turn out to be somebody else's alternative one as shown in Philip K. Dick's *The Man in the High Castle*. Nothing is fixed. But for the sake of convenience I will take ours as the default.

The Western Roman Empire didn't 'fall' in a cataclysmic event as often portrayed in film and television; it localised and dissolved like chain mail fragmenting into separate links, giving way to rump provinces, local city states and petty kingdoms. The Eastern Roman

Empire survived until the Fall of Constantinople in 1453 to the Ottoman Empire.

Some scholars think that Christianity fatally weakened the traditional Roman way of life and was a significant factor in the collapse of the Empire. Emperor Constantine's personal conversion to Christianity in AD 313 was a turning point for the new religion. By AD 394, his several times successor, Theodosius, banned all traditional Roman religious practice, closed and destroyed temples and dismissed all priests.

The sacred flame that had burned for over a thousand years in the College of Vestals was extinguished and the Vestal Virgins expelled. The Altar of Victory, said to guard the fortune of Rome, was hauled away from the Senate building and disappeared from history.

Roman senatorial families pleaded for religious tolerance, but Theodosius made any pagan practice, even dropping a pinch of incense on a family altar in a private home, into a capital offence. His 'religious police', driven by the austere bishop Ambrosius of Milan, actively pursued defaulting pagans.

The alternate Roma Nova timeline

In AD 395, three months after Theodosius's final decree banning all pagan religion, four hundred Romans loyal to the old gods, and so in danger of execution, trekked north out of Italy into the mountains. Led by Senator Apulius at the head of twelve prominent families, they established a colony based initially on land owned by Apulius's Celtic father-in-law. By purchase, alliance and conquest, this grew into Roma Nova.

Norman Davies in *Vanished Kingdoms: The History of Half-Forgotten Europe* reminds us that:

> *...in order to survive, newborn states need to possess a set of viable internal organs, including a functioning executive, a defence force, a revenue system and a diplomatic force. If they possess none of these things, they lack the means to sustain an autonomous existence and they perish before they can breathe and flourish.*

I would add history, willpower and adaptability. Roma Nova survived by changing; as men fought to defend the new colony, women took over social, political and economic roles, based on family structures. But given the unstable, dangerous times in Roma Nova's first few hundred years, daughters as well as sons had to put on armour and heft swords to defend their homeland and their way of life.

Service to the state was valued higher than personal advantage, echoing Roman Republican virtues, and the women heading the families guarded these values throughout the centuries. Inheritance passed from these powerful women to their daughters and granddaughters.

Roma Nova's continued existence has been favoured by high-grade silver in their mountains, their efficient technology, and their robust response to any threat.

Remembering the Fall of Constantinople, Roma Novan troops assisted the western nations at the Battle of Vienna in 1683 to halt the Ottoman advance into Europe. Nearly two hundred years later, they used their diplomatic skills to forge an alliance to push Napoleon IV back across the Rhine as he attempted to expand his grandfather's empire.

Prioritising survival, Roma Nova remained neutral in the Great War of the twentieth century which lasted from 1925 to 1935. The Greater German Empire was broken up afterwards into its former small kingdoms, duchies and counties; some became republics.

Twenty-seven years before the action of CARINA in the early 21st century, Roma Nova was nearly destroyed by a coup, a brutal male-dominated consulship and civil war. A weak leader, outmoded systems and a neglected economy let in a clever and ruthless tyrant. But with characteristic resilience, the families fought back and reconstructed their society while changing it to a more representational model for modern times. Today, the tiny country is one of the highest per capita income states in the world.

CARINA is a novella, a short novel, which tells the story of Lieutenant Carina Mitela's first overseas mission. In the Roma Nova series, it takes place between INCEPTIO and PERFIDITAS, the first two in the series. It reveals a regrettable incident mentioned in

PERFIDITAS and brings in favourite characters from some of the other books. But you don't have to have read any of the series to enjoy this story.

But I hope you'll be tempted to...

THE ROMA NOVA THRILLER SERIES

The Carina Mitela adventures

INCEPTIO

Early 21st century. Terrified after a kidnap attempt, New Yorker Karen Brown, has a harsh choice – being terminated by government enforcer Renschman or fleeing to Roma Nova, her dead mother's homeland in Europe. Founded sixteen hundred years ago by Roman exiles and ruled by women, it gives Karen safety, at a price. But Renschman follows and sets a trap she has no option but to enter.

CARINA – *A novella*

Carina Mitela is still an inexperienced officer in the Praetorian Guard Special Forces of Roma Nova. Disgraced for a disciplinary offence, she is sent out of everybody's way to bring back a traitor from the Republic of Quebec. But when she discovers a conspiracy reaching into the highest levels of Roma Nova, what price is personal danger against fulfilling the mission?

PERFIDITAS

Falsely accused of conspiracy, 21st century Praetorian Carina Mitela flees into the criminal underworld. Hunted by the security services and traitors alike, she struggles to save her beloved Roma Nova as well as her own life.

But the ultimate betrayal is waiting for her…

SUCCESSIO

21st century Praetorian Carina Mitela's attempt to resolve a past family indiscretion is spiralling into a nightmare. Convinced her beloved husband has deserted her, and with her enemy holding a gun to the imperial heir's head, Carina has to make the hardest decision of her life.

The Aurelia Mitela adventures

AURELIA

Late 1960s. Sent to Berlin to investigate silver smuggling, former Praetorian Aurelia Mitela barely escapes a near-lethal trap. Her old enemy is at the heart of all her troubles and she pursues him back home to Roma Nova but he strikes at her most vulnerable point – her young daughter.

INSURRECTIO

Early 1980s. Caius Tellus, the charismatic leader of a rising nationalist movement, threatens to destroy Roma Nova.

Aurelia Mitela, ex-Praetorian and imperial councillor, attempts to counter the growing fear and instability. But it may be too late to save Roma Nova from meltdown and herself from destruction by her lifelong enemy....

RETALIO

Early 1980s Vienna. Aurelia Mitela chafes at her enforced exile. She barely escaped from a near fatal shooting by her nemesis, Caius Tellus, who grabbed power in Roma Nova.

Aurelia is determined to liberate her homeland. But Caius's manipulations have ensured that she is ostracised by her fellow exiles. Powerless and vulnerable, Aurelia fears she will never see Roma Nova again.

ROMA NOVA EXTRA

A collection of short stories

Four historical and four present day and a little beyond

A young tribune sent to a backwater in 370 AD for practising the wrong religion, his lonely sixty-fifth descendant labours in the 1980s to reconstruct her country. A Roma Novan imperial councillor attempting to stop the Norman invasion of England in 1066, her 21st century Praetorian descendant flounders as she searches for her own happiness.

Some are love stories, some are lessons learned, some resolve tensions and unrealistic visions, some are plain adventures, but above all, they are stories of people in dilemmas and conflict, and their courage and effort to resolve them.

Printed in Great Britain
by Amazon

48672064R00080